After

The

Fire

T.K. Chapin

EMBERS AND ASHES - BOOK 4

AFTER THE
FIRE

Best Selling Author of " The Perfect Gift"
T.K. CHAPIN

After the Fire

DEDICATION

Dedicated to my mother,

the woman who taught me

that all things are possible with God.

CONTENTS

ACKNOWLEDGMENTS

First and foremost, I want to thank God. God's salvation through the death, burial and resurrection of Jesus Christ gives us all the ability to have a personal relationship with the creator of the Universe.

I also want to thank my wife. She's my muse and my inspiration. A wonderful wife, an amazing mother and the best person I have ever met. She's great and has always stood by me with every decision I have made along life's way.

I'd like to thank my editors and early readers for helping me along the way. I also want to thank all of my friends and extended family for the support. It's a true blessing to have every person I know in my life.

.

CHAPTER 1

Looking into the mirror that hung above the sink my wife, Denise, and I shared, I straightened the tie that hung around my neck. It was Sunday morning, my favorite day of the week. It not only marked the beginning of a week in the traditional sense, but it also served as the day of the week specifically set aside for God.

Church, God and the Bible had been my strength for decades. No matter how crazy the world got outside,

I knew on the inside that God and the Scriptures never changed. There was comfort in that fact, which my soul clung to and helped me to stay levelheaded for many years. From difficulties in marriage to losing a firefighter buddy and captain, God remained the same and helped me.

"Hey, Dad," Jasmine said from the doorway that connected the master bedroom to the en-suite. She was our eighteen-year-old baby girl who was now looking forward to graduating from high school in a few months.

I looked into those sweet brown eyes through the reflection in the mirror and raised my eyebrows. "What's up?"

"I'm not feeling so good . . ." She grabbed at her abdomen as she leaned into the doorframe, trying to lay on the dramatics.

I turned around and walked over to her. Placing one of my arms around her shoulders, I brought my other hand up to her forehead to check for a fever. "You don't feel warm. You sure? Or are you trying to get out of church again?"

She recoiled out of my grasp and furrowed her

eyebrows. "Why do I *have* to go?"

"We go as a family, dear, every week. You know that."

Jasmine had started pulling away from church about the time she turned eighteen. She carried that look of being torn between two worlds, one where she was free and one where she still wanted to please us. Each time I had a disagreement with her, I could see the desire for freedom burn in her eyes.

"Okay . . ." she said, walking away without another word.

"Come back here, please," I said.

She came back to the doorway. "What?" she asked, her chin dipped and her tone soft.

Using the tip of my index finger, I pulled her chin up to look her in the eyes. "I love you, Jasmine. I know you have a lot of emotions and . . . *stuff* going on inside of you right now. I know you want your freedom, and it will happen. You just have to wait."

Denise came into the bedroom and over to us. I smiled at her and looked back to Jasmine. "Your mother has been there too, dear. Doing the right thing and obeying us is going to pay off in the long run. You know that. The Bible speaks directly and plainly on such matters."

"I know, Dad," Jasmine replied as she wiped her eyes. "It's just hard. I'm going to get ready for church." She reached up and wrapped her arms around my neck, hugging me tightly. "I love you." She walked away and headed for the door.

Denise came over to me and said, "Our baby is going away to college soon, Micah . . ."

"I know. Speaking of, has she heard from Eastern yet?" I asked, turning and heading back into the bathroom to brush my teeth.

Denise followed me into the bathroom and shook her head. "When are you going to give that up? She doesn't want to go to that college. She didn't even apply."

"But she applied to Rowan University that's in what? New York?" I said as I stopped brushing.

"New Jersey. But yes, it's a really great fit. She liked the looks of it on the website."

"It just would have been neat to see her to go to Eastern Washington where you and I attended. I've been there—no website needed—it's amazing."

Denise smiled at me in the mirror as I put my toothbrush back in the holder. "That would be neat, and she'd be close."

I turned to her and nodded. "It's very close." I outstretched my hand with my palm up and said, "It's not clear across the country!" God pressed against my mind. Denise put her hand on my shoulder and rubbed my back a little as she smiled. "God knows what He's doing," she said.

"You're right."

After church let out, Denise and I took Jasmine out to lunch. On the drive to the restaurant, I looked in the rearview mirror and saw Jasmine staring blankly out her window. She looked like an inmate being taken out for an hour of outdoor time, not the little princess that I'd raised for the last eighteen years. Hoping to pry myself into her world, I spoke up. "How was youth group?" I asked as I looked at her reflection in the mirror.

She didn't say anything, just shrugged in the

slightest way possible to exert the smallest amount of energy.

Her coldness stung. Even though it happened more and more the older she got, it still hurt me every time it happened. What had happened to the Jasmine that was so easy to talk to? When she was younger, Denise and I could barely keep her quiet in the backseat after church. Now we'd be lucky to hear anything from her.

Taking a seat at a table in the restaurant, Jasmine sat directly opposite of us. She looked over at her mom and asked, "Could I have my cellphone back now? Still don't understand why I can't have my cellphone at church. I'm eighteen years old."

"She does speak," I said sarcastically.

Jasmine ignored the comment and Denise smiled as she pulled her purse up onto the table.

"You can't have it because you have to respect Joel and how he wants to run the youth group."

Denise looked through her purse for a few moments and then stopped. "I can't find it," Denise said, moving the purse back down to the seat beside her.

"What? Why?" Jasmine snapped.

"Hey," I said in a firm tone.

"What am I supposed to do now, Dad?"

I took a deep breath in and let it escape my lips as I took a moment for myself. I didn't appreciate the tone or attitude she was using. Leaning across the table, I motioned Jasmine to lean in. In a low and deep voice, I said, "Listen–you know you can't speak to your mother that way. You need to apologize, right now, Jasmine."

Jasmine leaned back into her seat. With a quick turn of her head, she looked at Denise and said, "Sorry."

"Thank you," I said as the waitress came over with our drinks. As she set the drinks down on napkins in front of each of us, I looked over at Jasmine and caught a glimpse of that rare smile on her face. It was the little moments like that which made all the painful moments more tolerable. God had blessed my wife and me with a beautiful daughter, and soon she'd be on the road to college.

CHAPTER 2

Cracking open my faithful Bible the next morning

in the dining hall at the station, I felt my mind and body begin to unwind and relax. There were still at least twenty minutes left before the other guys would start showing up for their shift. I needed God's promises more than ever after hearing a disturbing news report of more unrest in the Middle East on the way into work. My relationship with God through prayer and the Scriptures were like water to my soul. I needed Him.

Some people, like Ted at the station, found my lack of interest in the current affairs of the world and politics to be a sign of ignorance, but I counted it as obedience of what God's Word had instructed me to do. Philippians 4:8 was a passage I clung to.

Finally, brethren, whatsoever things are true, whatsoever things are honest, whatsoever things are just, whatsoever things are pure, whatsoever things are lovely, whatsoever things are of good report; if there be any virtue, and if there be any praise, think on these things.

While I have always stayed informed on major happenings, I always put God first and let Him lead my thoughts. With so much noise and chaos that goes on in the world, I couldn't imagine living any other way but by the Word.

Thumbing through my Bible, I came to the book of Job. My Bible study worksheet for Job marked the third chapter, which was the day's reading. Pausing, I folded my hands together to pray before starting in on my study.

Dear God. Thank you for this day and the time I have

to fellowship with you. Bless the reading and help me to see You through the words I digest today. Thank you for my family, job and co-workers. In your Heavenly name, I pray, Amen.

A depressing and gloomy read, I finished the chapter feeling bad for the guy. I pulled the worksheet out to start in on the questionnaire that went along with the chapter. The study wanted me to formulate a few sentences on what Job's point of view was of himself. Skimming back over the chapter, I came to the conclusion that Job wished he was never born. Leaning back in my seat, I put my hands behind my head and clasped them together as I thought about how it might feel to be at the point where I cursed my own birth.

"Freeman," Cole said as he walked into the dining hall from the kitchen with a cup of coffee in hand. My contemplative, emotionless face turned into a smile at the sight of Cole. Dropping my hands, I stood up and reached a hand out to shake his.

"How's it going, Brother? You're here a little early."

"It's going well," Cole replied, shaking my hand. He set his cup of coffee down and took off his jacket.

"Job study going okay?" he asked as he sat down and raised his chin as he attempted to peek at my worksheet.

"Yeah. How was your day off?"

"Good. Spent a lot of time with Megan and the boys after church," he replied. "Oh, and yesterday at Church the Youth Pastor approached me about helping out with the football team they're putting together for the summer."

"That's great," I replied. "You finally found something to do around the church."

"Yep. God's good." Cole smiled as she shook his head slightly and looked at his coffee. "God's good."

"Yes He is."

"Jasmine getting pretty excited to graduate? I saw that Denise already sent out the online barbeque invites for May."

I laughed. "Yeah. Little early for those invites, but at least she's on top of it. As for Jasmine . . ." I paused with a bit of hesitation in my voice. "Between last month being her birthday and June being only a few months away, she's burning to get out of the house."

"Hey, man. You raised a fine young lady. She'll do all

right in this world if she gets even a tenth of the wisdom you've fed her."

I nodded. "I know. I just worry about her being clear across the country when she hasn't ever been away from home for more than a few nights."

"God's in control, Freeman. You know that." Cole took a drink of his coffee and glanced down at the worksheet that was in front of me. "What's Job doing today?" he asked.

I smiled as I glanced down at the worksheet. "He's struggling pretty hard. Cursing the day he was born and all."

Cole nodded. "When I did that study I was surprised by a few of the questions. I'd never really done a study on Job before, and I learned so much through reading it again with a study aid."

"Yeah, I'm in that same boat. Read it before, but never with an aid. Pretty intense," I replied, picking up the papers. "And deep."

"I'll be honest. Kind of freaked me out that God let a good man get tortured like that. To let Job suffer so horribly . . ." Cole shook his head as he took another drink of his coffee.

Seeing Cole's concern drawn all over his face. I offered a word of insight I felt he needed. "God doesn't think like we do. We're limited in our ability to understand a decision or the impact of something that happens. Check it out. God knew Job would endure through it all because He could see into the future. He also saw the book of Job in the Bible inspiring believers for years down the line. God even knew at the moment of Job's suffering that you and I would be sitting here talking about it today. He sees beyond the temporary pain and has the entire picture in front of Him. It's all about how you look at the situation, you know? We have to keep our perspective broad, but our minds narrowly focused on God."

Cole's face softened and he smiled. "Smart, Freeman. Just like the funnel you told me about."

"Yep. Focused on God, we funnel everything in life through Him. Doing so helps us in our moments of weakness."

Cole and I chatted a bit longer before the rest of the guys showed up at the station. He had become one of the closest friends I'd ever had in my life.

The shift that day seemed to drag on endlessly. Only one call came in, around two in the afternoon, and it was a false alarm. After that call, Cole and I decided to go to a few classrooms at the nearby elementary school to teach fire safety. We arrived back at the station later in the day, had dinner with the crew, and then retired to our sleeping quarters after a relaxing evening of classic football games on the television.

We were all asleep when the siren in the room started blaring. Leaping from my bed, I hurried out the doorway with the rest of the guys and down to the bay.

As we suited up in our turnouts, Cole said, "We have a four-story fire down on Grant Avenue. There are multiple families trapped up top."

I knew what that meant. There was going to be a need for the aerial ladder. "I'll take the controls."

"Good," Cole replied. He went and jumped in the front of the engine truck to get his laptop fired up.

"I can do the controls if you want," Kane said.

"That's all right, McCormick. It's dark out, and by the sounds of it there are multiple families trapped." I pulled my suspenders over my chest and put on my coat.

"So?" Kane replied as he slid his hands into his gloves.

I paused and put a hand on his shoulder and said, "You have to pick the family with the most people to rescue first, or if they're the same sizes, decide who gets to be rescued and who has to wait. It can be nerve racking."

Kane went white as a ghost. I patted him on the shoulder and went around the ladder truck to get into the driver's seat. The aerial ladder was an excellent piece of equipment in our arsenal as firefighters, and while we didn't use it often, it was one piece of equipment you were happy to have when you did need it. I hadn't lost a soul using the ladder, but I had heard horror stories from the other stations about people dying in aerial rescues. That fear stuck with me every time I had to use it during a rescue.

Arriving at the scene, I glanced through the windshield and up at the flames as they reached into the night sky. The yellows, oranges and reds danced across the night. Cole and the rest of the engine truck crew were already there. Cole was busy telling people where to go while I was scrambling to find a good spot to park the ladder truck. If I positioned it too far away from the structure, there was a risk of not being able to reach the people. Too close would also jeopardize my ability to reach the people. Finally, I found the perfect spot. The only issue was that I'd have to roll the truck over two charged hose lines that were being used. It was never recommended to roll a truck over a fire hose, but when lives are in the equation, you sometimes don't have an option.

Getting on my radio, I radioed for Cole. "Taylor."

"Go ahead, Freeman."

"I'm rolling over two charged lines. Just a heads up."

I could see Cole look over at me through the windshield. "Copy that."

Moving the truck, I rolled carefully over the lines to make sure not to destroy the couplings. Just then,

the chief showed up in his car. He wore a pair of
blue jeans, a coat and a red Station 9 ball cap.
Walking straight up to Cole, he adjusted his cap as
he talked to him. Sometimes the Chief would
randomly show up to fires to watch how operations
unfolded.

After parking the truck, I spotted Kane across the
way as he seemed to be finished cutting the power
to the structures.

"McCormick, come here," I radioed to him as I went
to grab the wheel chocks that help to ensure that the
truck doesn't roll forward.

He jogged over to me at the truck as I slid the chock
under the front left wheel. "I'll get the stabilizers
going," he said.

I nodded up at him and he went to the back of the
ladder truck. Coming around to the other side, I saw
him check around the corner of the truck to make
sure it was clear and begin to extend the stabilizer
legs on the truck.

After I finished, I helped him set the stabilizers for
the truck.

Glancing up at the building as I climbed up the side

of the truck, I looked at the two families. One was a family of three; the other was only a man and a woman. Getting to the pedestal on top of the back of the truck, I made sure the hydraulic pressure was adequate before raising the ladder.

Kane stayed below on the grass behind me as I brought the ladder up and rotated it. I brought the ladder bucket down to the grass, and Kane ran over and leaped in. I began to bring him up and toward the first group, the family of three.

"Watch out for that tree," Cole said over the radio.

"I see it," I replied.

"Copy."

Keeping my eyes bouncing between the two different groups of people and Kane, I felt the sweat bead on my forehead under my helmet. I said a prayer for all involved. This job was the best job in the world most days, but there were a few moments when I had wished I'd never become a firefighter. The stress of it all weighed heavily on my conscience. Lives were sometimes put into my hands more times in a week than most people have in a lifetime. It felt like at least an hour, but it only took a few minutes to get Kane to the first family. He pulled them out of the structure and into the bucket. We got them safely lowered down to the ground. Paramedics were standing by as the family stepped out onto the grass. Hugs and tears flowed between the family members as they held each other closely. I spotted who I presumed was the father of the teenage girl in the group. He held her close to his chest as he wept and kissed her head.

Turning my thoughts back to the fire at hand, I sent Kane on his way over to the man and woman who were next to be rescued. Thankfully, the ground crew had been neutralizing much of the blaze and kept it from jumping to the other apartment buildings on both sides of the one that was on fire. Kane snagged the last two people we needed to rescue without difficulties, and we brought them down to safety. He made eye contact with me as he stepped off the bucket and gave me a nod.

I smiled. Kane was a good kid, and probably the youngest guy that I considered a friend. He had been a little lost in his early years with girls and partying, but since he'd made his recommitment to

Christ, he was a different man altogether.

"Good job, Freeman," Cole radioed.

"You mean good job, McCormick. He did all the work," I radioed as I smiled over at Kane.

"Yeah. Team effort," Cole said. "Let's hurry up with the rest of this fire so we can get some shuteye before the sun's up in a few hours."

CHAPTER 3

Arriving home the next morning, I walked into my house and could hear the sound of music blaring from the upstairs bathroom. Stopping at the banister, I glanced up the stairs and toward the bathroom. I could see through the cracked door that Jasmine was blow drying her hair and brushing it out while rocking out to her weird music. She must have sensed me, because the next moment she paused and kicked the door shut. Jasmine's coldness toward her mother and me was not the rosy picture I had envisioned some years ago.

Walking through the hallway and into the living room, I found Denise sitting on the couch with a cup of coffee in hand while she read over her women's daily devotional. Upon my entering the room, she set the devotional and coffee down on the end table to greet me. Getting up, she strolled across the carpet and up to me with a smile. "How was your shift?" she asked, touching my arm and kissing my cheek.

Setting my Bible down on the loveseat next to where I was standing, I shrugged and said, "It was good." Embracing Denise in a hug, I sighed.

"What's wrong?"

"Jasmine."

Denise pulled away from our embrace and said, "It's my fault she's cranky today."

"How come? Something happen?" I asked, walking over to the couch to sit down.

Denise headed into the kitchen as she replied, "She wanted to bring a boy over for dinner tonight. I told her I didn't think that was a good idea." Denise grabbed a cup from the cupboard.

Looking over at Denise from the couch, I said, "A new guy?"

Denise poured my coffee and returned to the living room. "Yeah. She seems love-struck." She handed me the coffee and sat down next to me.

Mulling it over in my mind, I was thankful that Jasmine respected us enough to bring him over instead of sneaking around. She might have been a little rough around the edges, but she still respected our rules. "She's eighteen now, Denise. We aren't going to be able to dictate her life for much longer. She'll be in college soon. Maybe we should have him come over for dinner. I'd rather have that than her sneaking around to see the boy or lying about going to a friend's house to hang out with him."

"Why would she do that? She respects us," she said, picking up her coffee and taking a drink.

"I don't know. I *feel* this is right thing to do, Denise. We don't want her resentment to build any more than it has already."

Denise sighed and glanced toward the hallway that led to the stairwell. "Okay. We'll have him over for dinner."

Taking a sip of my coffee, I said, "Had to use the aerial ladder yesterday on a call. Well, this morning."

Her eyes widened. "That's rare. Was that the Alpine fire on Grant?"

"Yeah," I replied. "There were two families trapped."

"Wow. The news said it started with a kid playing with a lighter?"

I nodded. "Crazy how fires start sometimes."

She smiled and reached a hand behind my back. She began to rub in a circular motion as she continued, "I'm proud of you working so hard at that job every day and providing for us."

"I know," I replied with a smile. "Thank you." My wife was the biggest blessing in my life. She was a woman like none other, and I thanked God for her daily. With raising Jasmine, work and even with my faith in God, Denise was always there to help sharpen me into the man of God I was meant to be. There were times in our marriage that were challenging, but those trials and pains only forced me to grow closer to God, and in turn, her.

Jasmine came down the stairs a few minutes later. She hurried through the hallway and headed into the kitchen when Denise caught her attention.

"Your father would like for your new friend to join us for dinner," Denise said.

Jasmine smiled and turned to come over and into the living room. "Really?"

"Yes, dear," I said. "Any boy my daughter has a fondness for, I want to meet."

"His name is Austin, and he's not a boy. He's a man," Jasmine replied.

My eyebrows furrowed immediately. "Oh?"

She came over and sat down next to me. She was still excited and her eyes were filled with hope as she looked at me. "He's twenty and he works down at Gordon's."

"The electronic store?" I asked.

"Yeah."

"What does he do there?"

"He unloads trucks. He's been doing that for over a year."

"Oh, wow. Cool."

"Way."

"I can't wait to meet him."

She smiled again and then looked over at her mom. "You both will love him."

"I'm sure we will," Denise said. Looking over at me, Denise continued, "You should make him your Chicken Alfredo."

"I can do that," I replied as I stood up and gave them both a nod. "I'm going to hit the shower and freshen up. This morning's workout was sweaty."

"Ew," Jasmine replied, standing up. "I'm going to school. Love you, Dad." She glanced over at Denise. "Love you, Mom."

Wrapping an arm around her, I hugged her and kissed the side of her head. "I love you, Princess."

Jasmine pushed me back, laughing. "C'mon, Dad. I'm not a kid anymore!" She began to leave. "See you guys later."

As she left through the hallway, I couldn't help but smile. My little girl was growing up, and I knew the years preceding were going to be some of the most important years of her life. The choices she makes now are going to be affecting her life forever.

Denise got up and came over to me. "Wonder if she

still plans to move across the country if she likes this guy?"

I shrugged. "She might be getting older, but she's probably not thinking a lot of things through like that. But hey, maybe there's hope she'll stay."

"Maybe . . ."

Hearing the worry in her voice, I looked into her eyes. "She'll be okay, no matter what. I promise."

She nodded and smiled. "Go get in that shower. You stink."

I let out a laugh and smelled my left armpit. "It isn't that bad."

She playfully pushed my shoulder and said, "Gross! I was kidding!"

Later that afternoon, I was in the kitchen dicing up the chicken I needed for the Alfredo that night when my cellphone rang. It was the Chief, Paul Jensen.

"Hello, sir," I answered the phone as I turned off the faucet from washing my hands.

"Freeman," he said. His voice sounded a bit broken.

I dried my hands on the hand towel and draped it over my shoulder as I turned around and leaned against the counter. "What's going on?"

The chief let out a long, drawn out sigh that sent my worry soaring. "I'm going in for open heart surgery next Tuesday."

My eyes widened and my chest felt like it was tightening as the words left his lips. I folded my arms together and brought my balled fist up to my lip. I knew he didn't know Jesus, and I had tried to speak with him about it years ago. He shot it down then because of how he'd watched his best friend's so-called 'Christian' father beat up his step-mom when he was a kid. Paul told me it was his only Christian influence and he didn't want anything to do with a religion that allowed that kind of person in. Knowing I had to proceed with caution, I asked, "Can we say a prayer for you?"

"I'd like that," he said. One of the toughest guys I had ever known in my life, I had only seen him upset maybe once—when we'd lost our captain, Thomas Sherwood.

I bowed my head and began to pray. "Dear Heavenly

and eternal Father in heaven. We come to the altar at which you sit and pray that you watch over Paul as he goes in for his operation next week. In the days leading up to it, I pray you show him the comfort and peace that only You can provide. Help his mind to stay calm and give peace to him and his family during this time. Thank you for sending your Son to die on a cross and rising the third day so that we can have this type of open communication with you through prayer. Thank you, Lord, for everything in our lives. We pray these things in your heavenly and precious name, Amen."

As I opened my eyes and lifted my head, I could hear Paul's voice soften as he spoke. It sounded much more relaxed. "Thanks, Freeman. I appreciate it. I'm starting to think more about this God of yours."

I smiled. "Oh, yeah?"

"Yeah. You, Taylor, Alderman and even the kid seem different than the rest at the station. You have a different way about ya'll that makes me wonder if I might be wrong about Christians. My wife has been a Christian for years, but she never really lived it out in front of me like you guys have."

"We're not perfect, but we do have something that others don't—hope."

The chief's wife called out to him. He covered the phone and began talking to her. A moment later, he came back to our conversation and said, "I have to go, but I want to catch a cup of coffee and learn more about the version of God you believe in."

"Sounds like a great idea, sir." My smile was from ear to ear upon hearing Paul talk that way. It didn't bother me that it had to come at a time where he was broken and hurt. That was the best type of redemption in my mind. Jesus didn't come to help the healthy, but rather the unhealthy.

"It'll be sometime after my surgery. And hey, just so you know, I haven't told the other guys at the station. Keep all this on the down low." I was a little worried that he was putting off the conversation to sometime after the surgery. Paul, like many of the people I had met along life's journey, felt he had more time. The problem with time is that we never know how much of it we have. My history with Paul stretched beyond Station 9. Back at my old station, he had come over to talk to the station's chief and found me in the parking lot admiring his '69 Chevy. We became instant friends after that conversation fifteen years ago.

After hanging up with the chief, I continued to prepare the meal for that night's dinner with a smile on my face and joy in my heart. Good ol' Jensen was finally coming around to the idea of God. What a wondrous day it was.

CHAPTER 4

Dinner was just about done when the doorbell

rang. Jasmine's eyes lit up at the sound. Leaping
from her seat at the kitchen table, she darted down
the hallway toward the front door.

Denise smiled as she brought the Alfredo saucepan
over to me and set it down by the noodles. As she
poured the sauce, she said, "Can you set the oven for
350 degrees? My brownies need to go in."

"Sure, honey," I replied as I stirred the sauce in with

a wooden spoon. Jasmine was talking a hundred words a second as she and Austin came into the kitchen. "Grab a chair, kids, dinner will be done shortly," I said smiling over at the both of them after a brief introduction.

"Okay, Dad," Jasmine replied. I turned back to the stove and finished stirring in the sauce and chicken. The aroma lifting from the Alfredo filled the air.

"That smells good, Mr. Freeman," Austin said as he took a seat at the table.

"It's a family favorite."

"The guys down at the fire station are absolutely crazy about it," Denise added.

"Station?"

"My dad's a firefighter," Jasmine said.

I nodded as I placed the lid over the pot of chicken Alfredo and then preheated the oven for Denise's brownies.

"Cool. So you run into burning buildings and whatnot?" Austin asked.

"Not exactly. I'm an engineer. I mostly drive the truck. There have been a few times I've helped elsewhere, but primarily I drive."

"That's cool, Mr. Freeman."

"You can call me Micah," I said, coming over to him to shake his hand. His grip was what you would expect from a twenty-year-old that was nervous about meeting parents—clammy and weak.

"All right . . . Micah," he replied, pulling his hand back from our shake.

The first look-over of the kid sat okay with me. His pants were around his waist instead of his butt, he had a clean haircut and no overgrowth of facial hair. Kid even had a job, according to Jasmine.

Denise got up a few moments later and put her pan of brownies into the oven. Then she came over to the table with the pot of chicken Alfredo.

Seeing the French bread still over on the counter, I jumped at the opportunity to help Denise. "Need me to grab the French bread?"

"That's okay. I got it, dear," she replied. She went back into the kitchen and retrieved the bread along with plates, napkins and silverware.

Once we were all situated at the table and had dished up our food, we bowed our heads to pray. I lead the prayer. "God, please bless this food for our bodies. Please bless the cooks that have prepared it and help us to enjoy this time getting to know Austin more. In Jesus' name we pray, Amen."

Lifting our heads, we all began to eat. Ten minutes into the meal, I thought of something to ask the boy. Finishing my bite, I wiped my mouth with the red cloth napkin that was in my lap and set it down on the table. Looking over at Austin and Jasmine, I looked at Austin and asked, "So you work at Gordon's, Jasmine said?"

He nodded as he scooped another bite up into his mouth.

"What's the plan when Jasmine goes to college in New Jersey?" I asked.

"Micah . . ." Denise scolded me. "Just let the boy eat!"

"Why would you bring that up?" Jasmine asked, setting her fork down.

My eyebrows raised as concern swept across me. "It's a *real* thing that you guys should be thinking about, right? The school year is about done, and New Jersey is pretty far away."

Austin looked over at Jasmine and then at me and Denise. In a soft and respectful tone, he said, "Sir.

Ma'am. . . it's a very good question. I haven't told Jasmine yet, but I've already spoken with Gordon's, and they said I could transfer to New Jersey if I needed to. In fact, there's a store near Jasmine's college that needs a night crew manager for stocking."

Fear surged through my veins as I saw glimpses of what I felt was the doomed future, living together off-campus and no way to help her escape if something went wrong with Austin. My face must have reflected the fear I felt, for in the next moment Denise grabbed my hand that was sitting on the table, jolting me out of my thoughts.

"That's awfully nice of them to offer that," Denise said, forcefully trying to break Jasmine and Austin's attention from me.

Jasmine nodded slowly and said, "It's going to be perfect for us."

My eyebrows furrowed and my stomach began to feel like it was twisting. "Please excuse me. I need to use the restroom," I said as I wiped my mouth with my napkin and set it down on the table.

The looks from both of my girls were ones of

suspicion, but I kept my quiet as I left the room and headed upstairs. I needed time with God. There was no way I could handle the realities of my daughter being so far away and alone with a boy.

As I walked past the bathroom, I felt bad for lying to them, but the truth wasn't one they wanted to hear. Walking into my room, I shut the door behind me and instantly began to feel better as the door clicked shut. Just a few moments alone were all I needed. Getting out of the situation without losing my temper was an achievement in itself. There wasn't much in life that could steal my joy away from me, but my princess making bad choices for her life was at the top of the list.

Lying down on the bed, I crossed my arms together and stared at the ceiling. I began to pray. I prayed for my daughter, my wife and for the future that was coming up fast. Without any other children in the home after Jasmine leaves and retirement just around the corner in another year, my mind often drifted to a singular question. What on earth was I going to do with all my time? I took all my anxieties and worry to God though. He was far better at handling it than I was. Committing my stresses and my newfound worry to the Lord, I finished out the prayer.

Sitting up, I stared at the doorknob for a moment as I contemplated returning to the dinner table. I didn't want to go back down there, but I knew I needed to. Denise was most likely down there scrambling for reasons why I hadn't come back down, and I felt the need to apologize. Taking a deep breath in and letting it escape through my lips, I glanced up at the ceiling once more.

"Help me, Lord," I said. Scooting myself off the bed, I headed back downstairs.

Finding Denise alone at the dinner table in the kitchen, I glanced into the living room to see if Jasmine and Austin were in there. They weren't. Coming over to the table, I sat down in my seat and Denise looked up at me with tear-filled eyes.

"Where'd they go?" I asked, reaching over to touch her hand on the table.

She pulled it back and shook her head as she wiped her eyes. "They left."

My lips pursed to form a thin line. "I'm sorry."

Denise laughed a little under her breath as she nodded. "How could you do that?" she asked as she got up and grabbed a couple of the plates from the table and headed into the kitchen.

"I just needed a moment with God," I replied, stacking the remaining plates on top of one another. Denise set the plates she had in the sink and returned back to the table to grab food. Pausing behind the chair Jasmine sat in, she rested her hands on top of the back of it and sighed. "It's a beautiful relationship you have with God, dear. It truly is, but you can't just walk out like that. Its hurtful not only to Jasmine, but to me. You left me here in an awkward situation."

Nodding, I said, "I understand that, and I'm sorry, Denise." I continued into the kitchen with the plates I had stacked. As I set them in the sink, I turned back to the table and asked Denise, "Where'd they go?"

"Erica's house," Denise replied, picking up the pot of leftover pasta that was still on the table. "Erica's going on a cruise tomorrow with her parents. They planned on going to see her after dinner anyways."

"Oh, wow. Really? Can she miss that much school? She's going to be graduating soon."

"Honey, I don't know," Denise replied coming into the kitchen. "I'm sure they figured something out. Don't worry about them."

I breathed a sigh of relief knowing they were at Erica's house. That was Jasmine's best friend in the world. They were both brand new to the school and church back when we first moved to Spokane, and the two of them became instant friends. Erica's parents were good folks and had been over for dinner on several occasions throughout the years.

"That was pretty crazy; he said he's going to transfer to be near her," Denise said to me over her shoulder as she began rinsing the dishes in the sink. She opened up the dishwasher and set a plate in before turning to me.

I nodded softly as I came over to her. Wrapping my arms around my wife, I looked deeply into her eyes. Smiling, I brought a finger up to her chin and said, "I don't like it . . . but God gave me peace about it all. He's in control and we have to remember that."

"He did put the stars in the sky," she replied as a

smile came over her face. She looked into my eyes and said, "How'd I get so lucky marrying you?"

"Must have been a mix-up," I replied, mirroring her smile. "Because I sure didn't deserve a woman like you."

"Shut up," she said, blushing as she playfully pushed me back.

I laughed and helped her finish loading the dishwasher before we tag-teamed the rest of the kitchen. Denise and I always worked so well together. It was a great reminder that God had made her just for me.

CHAPTER 5

All consumed in the book of Job the next day, I

jumped when Cole said my name as he walked into

the dining hall. I closed my Bible and put away my

worksheet to fully turn my attention to him.

"What's up?" I said as I pushed my Bible to the side

and brought my hands together on the table.

"You and I have a fun day ahead," he replied, sitting

down. "Hydrant maintenance."

"Man, I don't like doing that." I crossed my arms as

my lips pressed firmly together.

Cole laughed. "Chief handed the order down after B-shift broke a hydrant."

Nodding, I replied, "Seems to be the way it—"

Kane came sprinting into the dining hall. Sweat was pouring off his forehead and he was out of breath.

"What's wrong?" Cole asked, glancing past him.

Wiping the sweat from his forehead with his coat sleeve, he said, "My car broke down about a mile north of here."

"So you jogged the rest of the way? Why didn't you call for a ride?" Cole asked.

Kane smiled. "She said 'yes!' I couldn't think straight!"

Cole immediately jumped up and hugged him. "Congratulations! That's great. When's the big day?"

Kane's smile fell away. "Day?" He shrugged as confusion washed over him. "I don't know . . . I guess I didn't think about that."

Cole and I began to laugh.

"You didn't think about when?" I asked, looking at Kane.

He shook his head. "Was pretty focused on hoping

she'd say 'yes'." Kane squinted and looked at the floor as he rubbed the stubble on his chin. "Maybe in the summer? June?"

"Talk to your lady," I said. "She probably has something in mind. Summer is a fun time to get married. Do it outdoors."

Kane nodded. "Hey, before I forget: I'm going to get wood in the next week or so. Did you still need some?" he asked.

My eyebrows shot up. "Oh, man. Definitely. That's a little random, though." I laughed.

He laughed. "I've been meaning to mention it, but I keep forgetting. Anyway, I'll make sure to drop a truckload off for you after I get it." Kane pulled his cellphone out and began dialing as he left the room.

Cole turned around with a smile. "The kid sure is growing up, huh?"

I nodded. "I remember when he was just a young punk."

Cole sat back down. "Yeah. Times have changed quite a bit. Little Jasmine is graduating; my boys are going into elementary school." Shaking his head, he smiled and looked at me. "Just like Sherwood said . .

. blink of an eye and our lives keep changing."

"Yep. Don't forget that I'm going to be retiring in just a year, and I'll have an empty nest."

"Don't sound so down about it." Cole laughed. "I'd love to have a little silence. Boys are ridiculous."

"Speaking of boys . . . Jasmine's latest boyfriend informed us he's transferring to a place in New Jersey to be near her in the fall."

Cole's eyes widened.

"Yeah."

Cole sighed. "Well, does he go to church at least?"

Shrugging, I replied, "I don't know. Don't think so, or she would have told me that pretty quickly. She's a little rebellious, but I can tell she still desires to make me and Denise happy." I laughed. "To what degree, I don't know."

"Was that last boyfriend a church-goer?"

I nodded. "Yep. And it was the first thing she told us about him."

"Well I know that must be hard to hear; a boy is moving with your daughter. I couldn't imagine."

"I didn't like hearing it, that's for sure. I had to go pray about it immediately. Sometimes it can be difficult to trust it's all going to work out."

"I hear ya on that," Cole replied. "That's what we're called to do, though. God sees the big picture though we can't. You taught me that."

"I know," I replied with a short nod. Glancing over to my worksheet on Job, I said, "I'd better get the rest of this done before everyone else shows, and then we'll go do the hydrants."

"All right, Freeman," Cole said, standing up.

Later that day, around six-thirty in the evening, my wife, Denise, called. Excusing myself from the dinner table with the guys, I headed out into the hallway to take the call. She rarely called when I was on the clock.

"Hello?" I answered.

"Hi, dear," she said. Her words felt heavy. Something wasn't right.

"What's wrong?" I asked, stepping farther down the hall.

"Jasmine."

"What about her?" I asked, walking over to the steps that led down to the bay.

"She just stormed out of here with that boy!"

"Why?"

"She wanted him to stay here." Denise began crying. "I don't know what to do with her anymore, Micah."

"Wanted to stay where? At our house?" I asked, taking a seat on the top step.

"Yeah."

Cupping my hand over my forehead, I took a moment to ask God for strength. I kept quiet as I tried to process what was going on when Denise spoke again.

"I guess he got kicked out of the place he was staying."

"What? How's this our problem? What is Jasmine thinking?"

"I don't know." Denise sighed. "Jasmine didn't want to talk about anything. She just kept saying we're supposed to be Christians." Denise began crying again.

"She's coming back tonight, right?"

"I don't know . . ." she replied. "She was pretty upset

with me. I did the right thing, right?"

"Yes, dear. You did the right thing."

"Why does it *feel* like I did something wrong?"

"You don't want to upset Jasmine. It's natural."

"It's just hard! I want my baby back."

Getting off the phone with Denise, I returned to the dining hall and to the table to finish my meal. After eating, I headed down to the bay to mop the floors. Nobody really enjoyed doing the floors, but I volunteered to get a moment of silence. It was a chance to collect my thoughts and emotions and to talk with God.

As I scrubbed along the smooth bay floor, I prayed for God to help me understand how to deal with Jasmine. It troubled me deeply to have her months away from graduating and falling apart like she was. I asked God to help me understand how to do the right thing. As I dragged my mop along the floor over to the fire pole, I heard my name from above.

"Freeman," Cole said from the top of the pole.

Pulling myself out of the prayer, I glanced up and smiled at him. "What's up, Brother?"

"You okay?" he asked.

Hesitating for a moment, I looked at Cole and saw his desire to talk in his eyes. I could tell he sensed something was off about me and wanted to return the favor I'd done for him so many times before. "Things are rough at home."

"Let me grab a cola, then I'll come down," he replied and then vanished.

Allowing others into the difficulties I have gone through in the past was easy because the storm had passed and wisdom was able to be gleaned from it. But when it came to a storm I was in, I preferred to be alone with my thoughts and my God. That night my heart softened to let Cole in.

Cole came down the stairs and sat down on the last step. He looked over at me and said, "Come have a seat." He cracked open his can of soda as I set the mop down and walked over.

"What's going on?" he asked as I sat down beside him.

"You seem a little eager about getting up in my business," I replied with a hesitant laugh.

"I care about you and I consider you one of my best friends. You rarely talk about yourself and your own struggles of the heart. You're always the one helping others out. I'd love to return that favor."

Shaking my head, I said, "I talk about Jasmine from time to time. I know I've told you about some of the stuff that went on with Denise."

"Yeah, little things here and there, but for the most part you've been pretty even-headed. Remember when Sherwood passed away? Man, you were calm."

His question forced a wave of sad memories to wash over my mind as I said, "I do remember."

"You were a rock. Not just for me." He pointed back up behind him toward the stairs, "But for everyone here."

I nodded, but stayed quiet.

"What's got you so upset, Freeman?" Cole asked, taking a drink of his soda. "Jasmine?"

"You guessed it," I replied with a nod. "You know how I told you earlier that her boyfriend is moving across the country with her?"

"Yep," Cole replied.

"Well, now Denise informed me that they came over to the house and asked her if he could live at our house!"

"Oh, jeez."

"It gets worse. Jasmine was freaking out and kept asking Denise how we could call ourselves Christians."

"That's not good," Cole said, shaking his head as he looked down at his can between his hands.

"It's like all those years I raised her in the church and did all this parenting was in vain. She's just falling apart as she's about out of my house."

Letting out a sigh, Cole leaned back. "Life can get crazy. It's in these times that we need to rely on God to see what His plan is. Like this guy once told me, 'keep praying'."

A smile broke from my pursed lips as I recalled telling him that over and over again when he was going through struggles with Megan. "Sounds like someone pretty wise told you that."

He laughed and pushed my shoulder.

CHAPTER 6

When I arrived home the next day, I was happy to see my daughter's car in the driveway. I knew she had a late start that day for school because of a teacher in-service day. Looking up to the ceiling of my vehicle, I thanked God that she was home where she belonged. Denise never called me last night, so I figured everything must have worked out since Jasmine's car was there.

Walking in the front door, I could smell the coffee

brewing from the kitchen, and I smiled thinking of my lovely wife taking care of my needs. My appreciation for all she did swelled inside of me as I came down the hallway to the living room and kitchen.

I found Jasmine and Austin sitting on the couch watching TV in the living room, and I about freaked completely out, but the shock paralyzed me.

Denise quickly came over from the kitchen with a cup of coffee in her hand for me. Handing it to me, she said, "Can we talk?"

My eyebrows furrowed as my anger began to warm. This wasn't the understanding Denise and I had agreed upon the evening before. She grabbed at my shoulder and turned me away from the living room. Leading me into the hallway, I swatted her hand away from me. "Stop it," I said in a loud whisper.

"They can hear you, Micah. You stop it!"

I shook my head and said, "I don't care who can hear me, Denise. Answer me one thing. Did he stay the night here?"

"Yes."

I felt the chains that kept me calm and level-headed

explode at her words. As I turned to go back into the living room, she grabbed my arm again.

"What are you going to do, Micah?" Denise asked. Her eyes were fearful.

"Kick him out, of course."

"What about our baby? Our princess?"

Stopping, I got closer to Denise and looked at each of her eyes. "Tell me. What did they say to you to get you to flip so easily?"

Her lips closed and tightened as she hesitated to tell me. Then she said, "Hailee had a falling out with her daughter and didn't see her for over five years! I didn't want to risk that, Micah! Jasmine threatened to write us off!"

I brought my hand to my face and rubbed my chin and over my mouth as I gathered all my patience and strength not to lose my cool in the moment.

"Okay . . . but we have lines that cannot be crossed. They have to leave! Jasmine can stay and finish out the school year, but I doubt she will."

I turned to go down the hallway and Denise grabbed onto my arm, pulling me back. She looked me in the eyes and said, "Don't be mean, Micah. Don't sin in your anger."

"I'm done talking." I shook my arm free of her hold and went into the living room. Looking Jasmine in the eyes, I said, "Austin has to leave."

Austin shook his head and stood up. "You think you're a Christian?" he asked me, looking me in the eye. "You aren't anything but a hypocrite."

"You don't know what you're talking about, kid."

He laughed. "I know Jesus told you Christians to turn the other cheek, help people out. Stuff like that. Not kick your daughter out with nowhere to go."

"Jesus never said to condone sin, and the Bible—"

Jasmine interrupted. "Dad— don't. We'll go. I get it. I'll finish out my school year living elsewhere." With tear-filled eyes and a lowered head, Jasmine whooshed past me and up to her room to gather her things.

Austin tried to walk past me, following her, but I put a hand up to his chest and stopped him. "No."

"What's your problem? I just want to comfort her after you acted like a jerk."

"This is my house, Austin. You can go wait for her outside."

"Fine." He walked by, pushing his shoulder into mine.

Turning, I looked at Denise as she leaned her head against the hallway wall. Seeing her cry broke me into pieces.

"Yo. Babe. I'll be outside," Austin hollered up the stairs before going outside.

As the door shut, Jasmine came out of her room and hurried down the stairs with her backpack and a duffle bag.

"Honey," I said as she went for the front door.

She stopped at the door with one hand on the doorknob. Releasing it, she turned around. With tears running down her face and swollen eyes, she said in a broken voice, "What, Dad?"

My heart broke as I looked into her big brown eyes. Seeing her in pain tore me up inside. I didn't see an eighteen-year-old in rebellion; I saw a scared seven-year-old trying to fight for what she felt like she needed. "Your mother and I love you. You're always welcome to come back here. This is your home. And please, stay in school."

She wiped her eyes. "I already said I was going to

finish, don't worry about it. I just need to think right now. Clear my head. I'm not even entirely sure if I'm going to attend Rowan University anymore."

"What?" I asked. "And do what?"

She shook her head as she began crying more. "I don't know, Dad . . . I'll be at Jessica's tonight."

"With Austin?" I asked.

"Stop, Dad. Please!"

My heart ached. "Please just stay home."

"I'm eighteen. I'm leaving." She came over to Denise in the hallway and they hugged while they both cried.

"I love you, Jasmine," Denise said.

"I love you too, Mom."

She released from their embrace at the sound of her car horn outside, and I cringed. "Take care of yourself, Jasmine. Call us if you need anything."

As she wiped the tears from her eyes, I saw a little bit of a smile as she looked at me. It wasn't much, but for the moment it was all I had. She was my baby girl, and it ripped me apart inside knowing she wasn't going to be at home, sound asleep in her bed that night. Taking a step toward me, she wrapped her arms around my neck and said, "I love you, Daddy." She began to cry harder as she turned and hurried to the door, and then she left.

CHAPTER 7

A week came and went and before I knew it, the

day of the chief's operation had arrived. He had
requested me to join him at six that morning up at
the hospital. He wanted me to pray with him before
they took him back. He was scared of dying under
the knife.

On the way up to the hospital that morning, I
thought about Jasmine. She had been gone for about
a week, and we hadn't heard from her but once

when she called Denise asking about picking up more clothes. My little princess was making grown-up decisions whether I wanted her to or not. When Denise had her on the phone that one day she'd called, she couldn't get much information out of her about what was going on. She only said that they were doing okay and that she was still going to school.

When I got out of my car at the hospital, I was surprised to see Jasmine's softball buddy, Tessa, walking across the parking lot.

"Hey, Tessa," I said, shooting her a wave.

"Mr. Freeman. How are you?" she asked, walking over to me.

"Good. Hey. Have you talked to Jasmine lately?"

"Yesterday. I saw her at Jessica's house," she replied.

"Was Austin there?"

Her eyebrows went up. "You know about him?"

"Yeah," I replied, trying to keep my calmness so I could elicit more information out of her.

"He was there. Yes."

"I see . . ."

"Yeah. I can't believe he threatened his manager and

lost that job. Why would he do that?"

My eyebrows shot up.

"Oops," she replied. "I figured you knew that."

"What's their plan now if he lost his job?" I asked, stepping closer.

She backed up. "I don't know, Mr. Freeman. I should get going." Tessa turned and hurried to get into her car.

I turned and headed into the hospital. Worry began to settle within me as I thought about him not having a job. Did that mean she was going to skip out on college? I still held onto the hope that she wouldn't be that naïve. Walking inside the lobby of the hospital, I headed over to the receptionist desk and asked for Paul's room number. They sent me down the hallway to the elevators.

Stepping on, I turned around and hit the number three. Pushing the thoughts of my daughter aside, I focused in on Paul. I was there to support him, help him through this rough patch of his life. He could possibly die today on the operating table, and he needed Jesus.

Walking into his room, I immediately noticed the

sweat that was forming around his forehead. He looked worried and fragile. His wife, Lucille, sat down in a chair on the other side of the room as I approached him.

Grabbing a blanket that was pushed beside him, I dabbed his forehead. "You okay, sir?" I asked.

He laughed and pushed my hand away from his head. "You knock that *Sir* talk off. You're my friend, Micah."

I grinned. "Paul."

The nurse came in and gave us a five-minute warning before they were going to wheel his bed away to go prep. I could sense the nervousness grow as his eyes grew wide.

Looking at me, he said, "You ready?"

"Are you?" I asked.

"For what?"

"Well . . ."

"I know, Micah. I could die on that operating table." Paul shrugged as I saw his eyes begin to water. This was a man with eternity on his mind. He knew he could slip away. His hand trembled as it touched mine. "I don't have time left. I can't go get saved! I waited too long."

I reached my other hand down and put it on top of his. "Paul," I said, shaking my head. "There's nothing you need to do other than call on the name Jesus Christ and believe that he died on the cross and rose three days later. Confess with your mouth that Jesus is your Lord."

Paul tightened his lips. "C'mon, there's more than that, Micah! I have to get baptized and work in the church, tithe, stuff like that. I know the drill."

"No you don't." Crouching at my knees, I looked Paul directly in the eyes and said, "You have about two minutes before someone comes back into this room and takes you away, Paul. If you believe in Jesus Christ, you need to speak it and make this commitment right now."

"I believe." He looked up to the ceiling and began to cry. "I believe . . ." He let a long sigh that sounded relieving. "Salvation can't be that easy," he said, looking over at me with tears still running down his cheeks.

I put a hand on his shoulder and shook it slightly as I smiled. "Of course it's this easy. If we had to do something to earn our way into heaven, we'd fail. We are all fallen. Believing that you have some sort of ability to save yourself or earn your way takes away from the power of God. Paul, if you only trust that God has your best interest in mind, you'll find the peace you so desperately need."

He smiled at me.

"Mr. Jensen," the nurse said from the doorway, interrupting us.

"That's my cue," he said with a nervous smile. Looking over at his wife, she approached the side of the bed and I stepped out of the way. Watching as they embraced each other one last time before he'd be wheeled back, I smiled. It made me think of Denise. I held a lot of resentment toward her over the morning Jasmine left. I'd made her feel like she betrayed me, and while it wasn't right to allow them to stay over, it was petty in the grand scheme of things. Here was a man about to get his chest cut open, and he was clinging to his wife's hand on his way out of the room.

My thoughts drifted from Denise to the world and how so much of the world had become focused on temporary happiness like one-night stands, new relationships and binge watching of television shows. The world had it all wrong, though. True happiness was lasting relationships and moments like the one Paul was sharing with his wife.

Then the nurses wheeled Paul out the door and down the hall. Lucille stayed with him, clutching his hand, and I watched as they took him down to the operating room. She held on until they went through the doors and she couldn't hold on anymore. She looked almost helpless standing at the doorway that he vanished behind. I walked up beside her.

"Let's go to the waiting room," I said, putting an arm around her.

The hours were long as Paul's wife and I waited for the surgery to complete. It warmed my heart a few hours into the operation when his children showed up. They would have been there earlier, they said, but they had children to get to school.

Once the doctor came out and said everything was okay and that he was in recovery, I decided to leave Lucille with her family.

"I'm going to get going," I said, placing a hand on Lucille's shoulder as her children surrounded her.

"All right," she said, smiling up at me from her seat. She grabbed my hand that was on her shoulder and said, "Thank you so much for coming. It brought me great comfort to see him finally make that commitment."

I smiled.

"I was saved when I attended a youth camp years ago. A bit out of practice, but I'm saved by grace. I've always had a bit of a desire to go to church, but Paul never wanted to."

I nodded. "Maybe when this is all over, you guys can come to church with Denise and me. It's a good group of folks."

"We'll see. I tried once early in our marriage to get him interested in God, but he didn't want anything to do with it," Lucille replied. "There's a Baptist church up the road from us. Might go there. We'll figure something out. Thanks again."

"You're welcome. Take care," I said. Turning around, I headed for the door out of the waiting room and down the hallway to the elevator. Stepping in, I pressed the button for the ground level. Smiling, I looked up at the ceiling and praised God for the successful operation and the commitment of Paul. I could almost hear the angels singing in heaven knowing that a new soul was now saved.

Back at the house, I was pleased to see the pile of logs stacked alongside the house. Kane must have dropped them off while I was out, I realized, looking at them.

Going to the backyard, I went out to the pile of split wood I had stacked on the porch and grabbed the wheelbarrow. Walking back to the side of the house, I started hauling the wood. It took thirty minutes to get it all moved.

Then it was time to start splitting. Grabbing my axe, I put the first log up on the stump I used to split wood and took a deep breath in. The early March afternoon air was cold and crisp as it filled my lungs. I brought the axe up, and with one full motion I swung the axe, tearing right through the piece of wood.

Stacking the split pieces of wood, I heard a car pull up. Looking at my watch, I saw it was two in the afternoon, and Denise wasn't due to arrive for another hour, so I set my axe down and headed up front to see who it was.

Coming around the corner of the house, I saw Cole get out of his SUV. "Micah!" he shouted.

I knew something was wrong. He was tearing up and he said, "Get in. It's Jasmine."

Picking up my speed, I ran over to the car and got in. As he threw the car in reverse and gassed it, he said, "She's been in a wreck. It doesn't look good. I drove right over because you live so close to the station."

My world crumbled at his words. I covered my mouth as tears seeped out of the corners of my eyes. I began praying harder than I ever had before in my life.

Please, Lord! Please don't let anything happen to my princess! She's too young! She has so much ahead of her!

"She's up at Deaconess . . . I heard the call come in

over the scanner at the station."

"She's at the hospital. That's a good sign," I said. My phone buzzed. It was Denise. I answered.

"Our baby!" she shrieked.

"It's okay, honey. I'm going to the hospital right now."

My wife's wailing cries over the phone tore through me like a thousand pieces of shrapnel. And each sob was like salt being ground into an open wound.

"Amy, my friend that works at the hospital, said she might not make it," Denise struggled to add.

"Pray, honey. Let's keep on praying. God will help us."

"Okay," she replied. "How much longer until you're there? I'm heading there from the rec center downtown."

"I'll be there in a few minutes."

"I'll see you there. I want to start praying right now," she said.

"Okay. I love you. And remember, we serve an amazing and awesome God. He will come through."

Hanging up with Denise, my tears ran harder.

Cole was in the driver seat next to me talking, but I

couldn't hear anything he was saying. All I could think about was getting to my daughter. Bowing my head as I wept, I prayed fervently. The touch of Cole's hand on my shoulder brought little comfort in the moment, but it was better that he was there than nobody at all.

I got to the hospital before Denise and rushed to the emergency room's reception desk.

"My daughter is back there; I need to get back there! Where do I go?" I said in a loud voice.

The E.R. was relatively slow and the woman appeared startled as she reached over and pressed the button that controlled the swinging doors that led to the back. "Right through there, sir. She's in ICU, follow the signs."

I didn't even thank her; I just darted through the doors and down the hall, following the signs. Jasmine kept flashing through my mind. She was hurting and I needed to get to her. Hurrying to the first nurses' station, I spotted women standing behind the desk all nonchalant and chatting to one another. It irritated me that my daughter was hurt and they didn't care. "Jasmine Rae Freeman. Where is she?" I demanded as I approached the nurses' station.

"Only family can see her right now, sir. Are you her father?"

"Yes!"

"She's right over there. In room seven," one nurse said, pointing.

Going right to the room, I pushed open the door and went inside. It was like time stood still and everything became deathly quiet as I approached her hospital bed.

My little princess, I thought to myself.

A lump the size of a watermelon wrenched my throat shut as I looked at my daughter. Machines beeped and buzzed as cords and tubes ran everywhere. She was covered in bruises and cuts and her eyes were closed.

"Jasmine?" I said, coming to the side of the bed. Reaching down, I put my hand on hers. "Dear? Can you hear me?" I asked as my eyes welled with tears. Silence.

Tears fell down my cheek as I bent down on my knees and pushed her hair back. "Daddy's going to

72

fix this, Princess," I said. "I'm here now." I sniffed and wiped tears from my cheeks. Placing my hand on hers again, I rubbed her hand with my thumb as I continued, "You're going to be fine, and we're going to get you out of here and . . . get you to that college in New Jersey or wherever. Whatever you want to do, just wake up, princess, and I'll make sure you have everything you want."

My bottom lip shook as more tears fell down my cheeks.

"Sir, are you family?" a nurse asked, coming into the room.

I stood up and looked at the nurse. Wiping my eyes, I said, "Yeah. So what's the deal? Where do we go from here?"

"Let me get the doctor," she said.

Denise came in as the nurse left and ran over to the bed. Sobbing, she hugged Jasmine as she said, "My baby!"

My heart was breaking and I looked up at the white ceiling in that hospital room. Praying, I asked God to help. I asked for Him to step in and help Jasmine. But as I prayed, I felt I already knew what the doctor was going to say. Between what Amy had told Denise and the countless tubes and machines, it wasn't going to be good.

The doctor came in the room and lowered his clipboard to his side as he removed his glasses and dropped them in his coat pocket. "You're Jasmine's parents, correct?"

At our nods he continued, "Okay, so she was in a car accident. She was unresponsive when she arrived and we took her straight into surgery to try and save her, but it didn't go well. She's on life support right now."

"Okay. How long does she need to be on that before we can take her off and she'll be able to go home?" Denise asked.

I put my arm around her shoulder and brought her in close to me.

The doctor shook his head. "There is no easy way to say this . . . Jasmine doesn't have any brain activity. She's already gone in the most important way. We'll continue to do basic brain and body checks for the next six hours, but I am not hopeful for the outcome. I believe it's time to let her go, she's not here anymore."

I sniffed again as I began to sob. I looked over at Jasmine on the bed. Denise began sobbing hysterically and I held her tighter as tears poured down my cheeks and hers. My baby girl, our princess, was dying.

"A decision will have to be made soon if you would like to donate any of the remaining healthy functional organs, I know no one wants to talk about that, but to save a life from this tragedy sometimes helps us heal ourselves," the doctor said. "I'll be back in a bit to see what you have decided."

Turning to Denise, I brought my hands to her arms and rubbed them gently. Looking into her eyes, I cleared my throat and pushed out, "Jasmine's going to be with Jesus today, honey."

Denise let out a hopeless cry as her words strained. "I can't lose my baby! Please, Micah . . . Please don't."

"I don't want to lose her either." I struggled to continue. Wiping my eyes as the lump in my throat tried to close off my breath, I said, "But it's her time, Denise."

"Why?" Denise asked as she clenched onto my shirt. "Why her?"

"It's God's timing, not ours." I had said the words before and believed it, but this time it just didn't make any sense to me. I said it because Denise needed me to, because it's what I was supposed to say. But I didn't feel those words to be true this time. Looking over at Jasmine again, I could see all the hopes, dreams and future she had before her fade. Putting my arm around Denise, we walked over to her bed as we continued to cry.

CHAPTER 8

Sadness didn't begin to describe the drive home from the hospital that day. Donating her organs didn't help me heal, but I knew Jasmine wouldn't want her death to be in vain. There was a sense of hopelessness in the air that Denise and I shared that evening. Denise stayed silent as her eyes remained fixed out the car's window, and tears continuously streamed down her cheeks. I was powerless over the pain that we both shared, but I longed for something I could do to ease hers.

Denise's phone buzzed in her purse that sat near her feet on the floorboard. She ignored it—she might not have heard it. I had no idea what was going on in her mind. Then it buzzed again.

"Why won't people just back off?" I asked in a soft tone as I turned onto our street.

She sniffed and shook her head, keeping her eyes fixated out the window. She managed to push out a reply, but it was laden with grief. "I don't know . . ."

My jaw clenched as I thought about the outpouring of love and support from loved ones and friends. It was sweet, but we just needed space and it felt like nobody understood that.

Her phone began ringing and she sighed heavily. She grabbed her purse and pulled it up onto her lap. Looking at the screen, she said, "It's my mother." She slid her finger across the screen and ignored it.

"Why'd you ignore it? She probably wants to know what's going on."

"I can't do this!" she finally snapped at me. "I can't deal with this right now, Micah! I need to breathe!" She started crying harder and choked up as she continued, "My baby girl is dead, and I don't know how to process this right now."

"Can I see your phone?" I asked, being sure to keep a soft tone.

She pulled it out of her purse and handed it to me as I parked her car in our driveway. Holding the power button, I said, "There. Take your time to process this. I'll take care of the rest."

She shook her head as she looked over at me. Her red and swollen eyes made contact with mine for the first time since we got in the car. Those once lively and sweet eyes reflected a sorrow so heart wrenching that it cut into the deepest parts my soul. I know she didn't want to talk, but she did say something that touched me. "Thank you, Micah." I loved her ability, even in the midst of grief, to acknowledge and appreciate the things I did. Grabbing her purse and phone, she got out of the car.

I watched as Denise went around the front of the car and up to the house. Her shoulders were hunched and her head hung low as she climbed the steps to the front door. Looking up at the house, it seemed so different than only a few hours ago. It wasn't a home anymore, just a reminder of a life lost. Even the way Denise shut the door came across as sad. Everything felt sad. When the front door finally shut, I let myself fall apart in the car. Tears ran violently down my cheeks as I slammed the steering wheel. My anger boiled as I bowed my head to pray.

Dear Lord, how am I going to help my wife, Lord, when I can't even help myself? She's hurting and broken, but I'm not doing so hot either. I don't know what to do.

I paused my prayer and looked up at the house again. A whisper from the depths of my soul told me I couldn't do this.

I pushed the whisper aside, writing it off as my flesh torturing me. Opening the car door, I went inside the house. As I shut the door behind me, I heard my bedroom door upstairs close. Giving her some space, I went into the living room and pulled the laptop out from beside the couch. I knew what I needed to do. There had to be some sort of message sent out online to pull the focus off Denise and to bring it all to an understanding of what had happened and what we need from others. I had phoned my father earlier at the hospital and he trickled it through the family, so it was getting around, but I needed a statement from us sent out to all our friends and extended family. Denise and I were fairly active in the church, so it'd be good if others knew what was going on.

Staring blankly at the little window where I updated my status, my tears began to flow again. Clenching my jaw, I forced the tears to stop and my fingers were soon gliding across the keys. There were ten solid minutes of typing and backspacing and then typing some more. *There's no right way to do it*, I thought to myself as I wiped my face of tears. Taking a deep breath, I set my fingers on the keyboard again and began typing.

Tragedy can strike in a moment we least expect. It comes like an unwelcomed guest into our lives and challenges us like nothing else. Today we lost our baby girl in a car accident. While we know she's with Jesus now, we can't help but wonder *why*. How can a loving God take away a

life before it truly began? She was on the brink of graduating high school, going to college and starting her life. While at the hospital, I watched as some knocked-up, teenage girl was wheeled by to go deliver a baby out of wedlock. That infuriated me. How could some stupid, knocked-up teenager get to keep on living while my sweet angel dies?

Realizing that wasn't the right thing to say and almost embarrassed by my harshness, I backspaced it all out. I was tired of trying, so I went ahead and did a very plain and dry status update that delivered the facts and helped those who read it be comforted.

Today Jasmine was in a fatal car accident, and we ask for your prayers and distance while we grieve the loss of our daughter. It's through trials and loss that we are able to truly rely on God Almighty and all His infinite power. God is good, and we will praise Him in this storm. Jasmine will not feel the pain of this world anymore, only everlasting joy as she is in

Heaven now with Jesus. Thank you for your condolences and we appreciate the distance for us to grieve during this time.

It felt fake, real fake. But I knew it's what people needed to hear from a deacon in the church and the wife who helps lead a Sunday school class every week. They didn't need to know the truth and the absolute struggle I was having internally at the moment. They needed the encouragement.

Hitting 'submit', I closed the laptop and turned off my own phone so I could ignore the incoming calls, text messages and notifications that I knew would follow even though I had specifically requested distance.

Glancing through the hallway and to the stairwell, I thought about Denise upstairs. Knowing she was hurting, struggling, and depressed, I felt inclined to at least poke my head in there. There weren't words I could say or any action I could do to help, but maybe my presence alone could be of some benefit to her.

Climbing the stairs, I paused at the top as my eyes

fell on Jasmine's bedroom door across the hall from ours. I felt that same lump from the hospital in my throat and anger in my heart. I clenched my jaw as emotions ripped through me and tears began to fall again—anger at God, sadness over the loss, and a great sense of confusion as to why it all had to happen.

I took large and quiet breaths to not alert Denise. I had to keep it together for her. I had to be strong for her. She needed a man of strength who could be there for her in her time of need.

Once composed, I walked to our bedroom door and opened it. Seeing Denise lying on the edge of the bed and facing the wall about killed me. She was miserable. "Denise," I said, taking a step inside.

"I came up here for a reason, Micah . . ." she said in a quiet voice. "I need to be alone."

"Okay. Is there anything I can do or get for you?"

She sat up and turned around. Her eyes were still swollen and tear-filled. "How about our daughter? Can you get that for me?"

"Denise . . ."

"Oh. You can't do that . . . can you? You, with that

great relationship with God. What good is that now, Micah? My baby is dead! He could've kept her safe! He should've watched over her! He failed her and He failed me!" She shook her head and looked over to the lamp that was on the end table. She stood up and touched the rim of the lampshade and then suddenly grabbed it. Yanking the cord out of the wall, she launched the lamp across the room. I ducked and it crashed into the wall behind me, shattering. "Leave me alone!" she yelled.

I turned and left the room, devastated at the temper my wife had succumbed to. Tears filled my eyes as I closed the door.

CHAPTER 9

The week following the accident flew by, but not without moments that were grueling and long. Off and on our friends, family and people from church came by the house to bring meals and to see how we were doing. Even a few of the guys from the station stopped by a few different times during the week. One early afternoon the doorbell rang. I got up from the couch with a heavy sigh and headed for the door. Stopping at the stairs, I hollered up to Denise, who had camping out in the bedroom. "Were you expecting someone?"

She came out from the room and rested her hands on the railing as she looked down at me. "No."

I grunted and continued to the door.

"Move a little quicker, please. I don't want to stand here longer than need be. And I swear, if it's Mrs. Roberts from up the street again, I'm going to lose it."

I opened it. It was our pastor. "Pastor," I said, surprised.

He put his hands up and said, "I know you weren't expecting me, but I wanted to chat with you guys."

"I don't want to chat," Denise said coldly as she turned and went back into the room. I could almost see the pastor cringe as the bedroom door slammed shut.

"She's a little upset," he said as I motioned him in and led him to the living room.

"You could say that," I replied in an emotionless tone as we sat down on the couch. "Our daughter *is* dead."

"We've been praying for you. We're all really sorry

about what happened."

I laughed a little and shook my head as I wasn't able to mask my true feelings in the moment. Praying for me? Sorry about it? I was sick of hearing the same thing over and over again from every person I spoke with since Jasmine had passed.

Are you upset with God, Micah?" he asked, sitting down on the loveseat as I took a seat on the couch.

My eyebrows furrowed and I said, "How could you ask that? You know I know the Bible inside and out."

"I'm not asking about what's in the Bible. I'm asking about what's inside of you."

My jaw clenched and I peered toward the hallway, thinking about Denise. "I am upset. I have a lot of anger and confusion right now. I can't stand not knowing the reasons for this."

"Remember when your captain died?"

"Of course," I replied, sitting back into the couch.

"You struggled, but you understood it's God's timing and He is ultimately in control."

"Yeah . . . but this is my daughter. She had her whole life ahead of her." I shook my head as tears welled in my eyes. "The Cap had lived a long life. Had grown kids. It was hard, but it was okay. My daughter, though . . ." My lips tightened.

"Thomas was still someone's husband, someone's dad, and even someone's kid."

"Good point, but he wasn't any of that to me, Pastor."

"I know," he replied with a raised eyebrow. "But you were walking around counseling everybody with the loss."

"I don't get the point you are trying to make."

"The point I'm trying to make is God's timing is God's timing regardless of the relationship with the person who passed on."

"I know that, but that doesn't mean I like it or understand it."

"You and I have promises in the Bible we can rely on. We have hope."

"God promises a lot in the Bible. Some of that is where my confusion stems from. Like for instance, He has great and wonderful plans for our lives. That's a pretty interesting promise, especially for Jasmine. She's dead, yet the moronic boyfriend gets to live. Wonderful plan, God!"

"Micah Freeman!" the pastor scolded me as he stood up. "I've known you for a long time, and I would never expect to hear these kinds of things from you. You are a man of God!"

He was right; this wasn't like me at all. I was the cool and levelheaded guy that was always calming people down when they were upset. I took a deep breath and raised a hand to my forehead. Rubbing my temples with my hand over my brow, I said, "I'm sorry, Pastor. I don't know what to do."

"Go."

"What? Where?"

He came over to me and put a hand on my shoulder. "Back to Calvary's Cross. Get back to basics. This . . ." He paused and looked me over before continuing. "This isn't you." He dropped his hand away from my shoulder and headed out of the room and down the hallway.

Knowing I needed time alone with God, I caught up to him before he left out the door. I said, "Would it be bad if I left town and went to my cabin?"

He glanced over at the stairs for a second and then at me. "I wouldn't leave your wife; I'd take her." He forced a smile out of the corner of his mouth. "Pray about it."

I reached out and grabbed onto the doorknob to open it for him. As he stepped outside and went to his car, I thought about Denise. She was hurting and miserable just as much as me. My gut told me I shouldn't want to go on the road trip to Ocean Shores, but I knew I couldn't stay in this house for another night.

Closing the front door, I headed upstairs. Praying as I climbed my way up the stairs, I asked God for peace to wash over Denise and for Him to help her heart soften.

I opened the bedroom door and found Denise asleep under the big white comforter on the bed. Coming into the room, I took a seat on the edge of the bed next to her. Pushing the hair out of her eyes, I glided my fingers softly across her cheek. She woke up.

"What are you doing?" she asked with furrowed eyebrows.

"Stop being so mad."

"You woke me up to tell me that?"

"No. I'm going to head out to the cabin."

She sat up and looked at me. "What? You're going to Ocean Shores?"

"Yeah. I want you to come with me."

She scoffed and looked away. "Running away from my problems isn't something I'm interested in, Micah. I, unlike you, can deal with them."

My eyes strained as I kept my lips sealed. I didn't even say a word, and she knew exactly what I was thinking.

"Shut up, Micah!" she demanded. "I know what you're thinking. I've kept myself hidden away up here in the bedroom. How's that for facing problems? But you know what? I'm not leaving town with you. I need to deal with me alone too. I think—"

"I think your bitterness and coldness froze your heart, Denise." I raised my hands and stood up from the bed. "I'm not forcing you to go. I wasn't just going to walk out of the house and leave without letting you know my plans and asking you to come with me." I let my hands drop to my sides and I headed over to the closet to start packing.

As I pulled the suitcase down from the shelf up in

the closet, Denise spoke up again. Her tone was softer this time; I don't know what changed. "Why are you going?" she asked.

Turning around as I set the suitcase down on the floor of the closet, I looked at her. "I want to be alone with God. Go back to the cross of Calvary and get back to basics." I shook my head and looked around the room. "Everything here is a reminder of Jasmine."

"This isn't something you can escape. This is real. Our daughter is dead."

"Yeah. Stop saying that all the time. I know she is. I need to get myself re-aligned with God, Denise."

"You'll never find a reason *why*, Micah, if that's what you're searching for."

I paused.

"And you already knew that."

My lips pursed and my jaw clenched as I turned and began pulling shirts and pants down from hangers. "I really don't understand why you need to go on this trip, but whatever. If you *need* this, then do it." She hid back under the covers and went silent.

I stopped packing and walked over to Denise's side

of the bed and bent a knee down. Pulling the covers down from her face, I wiped a runaway tear from her eye. Taking her hand in mine, I kissed the top of it and looked her in the eyes. "Why the change of heart?"

"I don't want to be the she-demon I've been the last week. If you die in a car wreck today, I don't want that to be the last thing you remember."

"Oh," I replied with a raised brow. "Romantic."

She forced a smile but said nothing in return.

"I'd love for you to join me."

She sniffled. "I don't want to go. I have absolutely no desire."

"Well, if you change your mind, you'll know where I am."

"How long are you going to be gone?"

"I don't know," I replied, standing up and walking over to the window that looked over the front yard. Glancing out the window, I said, "As long as it takes."

"Okay," she replied. "Did you pray about it?"

Turning around to her, I nodded. "Yes. and I have peace about it."

"You should go. I don't like it, but I think you should go."

"Thank you." Going back into the closet, I finished packing my suitcase.

Giving Denise a kiss on the lips, I said, "I'll call when I arrive there safely, but you know you can always call me if you want to talk." I headed downstairs and out the front door in pursuit of the cabin at Ocean Shores.

CHAPTER 10

Six and a half hours later I arrived in Ocean Shores.

When I pulled into town it was about dinner time, so I headed down to my local favorite restaurant, The Home Port. They had the best fish and chips in town.

Getting out of my truck, I inhaled a deep breath of the ocean air. I felt relaxed. Sadness still lingered, but the salty ocean air had a way of just setting me at ease. The ocean itself always reminded me of how big God was. Walking up to the front doors of the restaurant, I smiled at a couple as I held the door open for them.

Once inside, I spotted Joe Edmunds sitting at a table with his wife, Betty, and their two kids, Lonnie and Quin. The Edmunds were a family we knew from the local Christ Community Church and lived only a few houses down from the cabin. We had met them a few years ago when we first got to town. Denise, Jasmine and I always visited them when we came to town. This wasn't one of those trips, though; I wanted to be alone.

I was glad when they seemed to not notice me and the hostess led me to the opposite side of the restaurant. "Your waitress will be here shortly," the young woman said as she set the menu down and returned to the front.

The atmosphere inside The Home Port was lively and the aroma of fried fish could be smelled everywhere in the restaurant. Light country music played in the background, but it was mostly drowned out by the conversations at the tables. Opening my menu, I already knew what I wanted, but I wondered if they had anything else that might pique my interest.

"Could I get you started with a drink? Tonight's special is a Long Island Iced Tea for a buck," the waitress said.

"Just water with a lime would be great," I replied, looking up at her with a smile.

"Okay. Any appetizers?"

"Nope."

"Okay. I'll be back with your water," she replied with a smile as she left the table.

Returning to my menu, I continued to flip through the pages.

"Micah Freeman?"

Looking up, I saw it was Joe.

"I thought that was you!" he said. "It's not summertime yet, what you doing here? Where's the family?"

Recalling when I first met Joe, I remembered that he doesn't use the internet or a smart phone. There was no way I was going to explain to him what had happened in the middle of a busy restaurant, so I slid away from the truth without entirely lying about it. "They didn't come this time. I'm just here taking care of some stuff."

"Ahh . . . Getting the cabin ready for the summer? I remember Jasmine talking last summer about coming up with her friends after graduation."

Hearing her name used in the future tense about made my heart stop. I shook my head and said, "I . . ."

The waitress arrived back at the table and set my cup of water down.

Joe patted my shoulder and said, "I'll see you around." He went back to his table, relieving me of the conversation.

"What'll it be tonight?" the waitress asked.

"Fish and chips," I replied, picking up my menu and handing it to her. My eyes stayed fixed on Joe as he returned to his table and sat down. Watching Joe laugh and enjoy time with his family was unsettling. That whisper from inside of me spoke up again, telling me I couldn't handle all of this. I shook the thought away and picked up my glass of water.

I got to the cabin around seven and walked in the front door. Memories flooded my mind from the last time I had visited with Denise and Jasmine. It was last summer, for an extended weekend getaway. Setting the keys down on the dusty counter in the kitchen, I looked over at the sink. I thought about Denise laughing there and smiling as Jasmine sang and danced around the living room. I grabbed onto the back of a chair at the kitchen table as I felt myself weaken. My legs wanted to give out, along with the rest of me. This was supposed to be an escape from the memories, but it was just more of them.

Lifting my eyes, I glanced out the window that was just beyond the table. Able to see a part of the ocean, I took a breath. God created that ocean by speaking it into existence, I told myself. He's bigger than my problems. I wiped a runaway tear.

Turning my attention over to the kitchen, I went and grabbed a wash rag from a drawer and began wiping down everything with a surface. Once done, I headed down the hallway to the laundry room to toss the rag in the dirty clothes hamper.

On my way back out, I saw Jasmine's room.

I lost it.

Tears welled in my eyes and my jaw clenched as they made their escape and began running down my cheeks. I dropped to my knees and brought my hand up to the door.

"Why, God? Why'd you do this?" I asked, looking up at the closed door. "What purpose did this serve?" My thoughts drifted to Denise. "My wife is destroyed, my daughter is dead, and I'm left wondering *why*?"

My throat felt as if it was closing. Covering my face, I dipped my chin to my chest. Shaking my head, I said, "God. This makes no sense . . ."

A knock from the front door startled me out of my breakdown. Jumping up, I wiped my eyes and took a few deep breaths to collect myself. Going to the front door, I glanced through the peephole—it was Pastor Clarkson from Christ Community.

I undid the deadbolt and opened the door.

He smiled. "Micah," he said.

I opened the screen door and said, "Come in, Pastor

Clarkson."

He stepped inside and we went into the living room.
I sat down in the recliner while he took a seat on the
couch. I watched as the pastor's eyes traveled across
the room. He seemed rather curious. "Joe told me
you were in town," he said as his eyes arrived back at
me.

"Yep." I raised my hands out to both of my sides and
said, "Sure am."

"You going to be here for a while?" he asked with a
raised eyebrow.

I shrugged. "I don't know yet."

"Joe said you didn't bring the family. He didn't seem
to know about the accident, but don't worry, I didn't
tell him."

"Thanks."

"Where's Denise?"

"Home." Realizing I was being curt, I felt bad. "Sorry
if I'm being a little short. I just really came out here
to be alone. Trying to stay under the radar a bit."

He nodded. "I understand." The pastor slapped his
knees and stood up. "Well, I hope we see you on
Sunday. I won't keep you."

"We'll see." The last thing I needed was more people trying to say they're sorry for my loss. Some of them had to already know about Jasmine. Sensing my annoyance with the pastor, I questioned it. Why did I feel so angry? So annoyed?

The pastor flashed another smile and asked, "Remember last summer when you filled in for me at the church when I was out of town?"

"How could I forget? I stumbled through the entire message."

"Oh, c'mon, Micah. You did great. People still talk about the story of that grocery store fire you told and how God is always with us in storms."

I forced a smile.

We walked over to the front door for him to leave and he extended a hand. "If you need to talk, let me know."

"Thanks."

Shutting the door, I went back into the living room and sat down on the couch. Dropping my face into my palms, I began to cry. Praying out loud to God, I pleaded for His help.

"Take away this anger, this disdain I have for

everybody I see. Let my joy return and allow me to have pleasure in my heart for You, Lord. Help me."

After the tears subsided, I remembered I'd told Denise I would call her and let her know I made it to town.

"I made it safe," I said.

"That's good. Did you go get yourself some groceries?" she asked.

"Not yet. I just stopped in at The Home Port for dinner."

"Mmm . . . Waffle Supreme," she replied.

"You sound a little more chipper."

"I got up and did some laundry, took a shower. It really helped."

"Wow. That's great to hear. Hey, guess who was at The Home Port?"

"Who?"

"Joe Edmunds and his family."

"Oh jeez. He loves you."

"I know. He's ridiculous." I sighed. "I'm still wishing you were here."

"I think some time alone to process this is good for me. I don't want to break down every ten minutes in front of you."

"But I'm okay with that, Denise."

"That doesn't mean I'm okay with it. This is good. I shouldn't have gotten upset with you earlier for wanting to go out to the cabin. I'm sorry I did that."

"It's okay. I feel kind of dumb coming all the way out here."

"Why?"

"I don't know. I wanted to be alone and I'm not. I know Joe's right up the road. The pastor even came over already. I envisioned it a little differently. Guess going to The Home Port was a bad idea."

"Don't beat yourself up about it. You would have seen people at the store. Just go with it."

"Okay."

"As for church, I'd just tell him you're not going to come. Don't over complicate it. That's my job," she replied with a little laugh.

Wow, I thought to myself. *She's laughing?* Maybe being away was really good for her. Then, a moment later, she was crying.

"What's wrong?" I asked, adjusting my seat on the couch.

She sniffled and said, "I feel guilty."

"For what?"

"Laughing."

"Why?"

"I don't feel like I should be happy at all. It feels wrong."

I looked down at the hardwood floor in the living room and said, "I know the feeling. But it's not right. We shouldn't feel that way. Jasmine wouldn't want us to be miserable."

"I need to go," she said with broken words.

My eyes filled with tears as I replied, "Okay."

Wiping my eyes after I got off the phone with Denise, my phone began to buzz. It was a text from Cole wondering where I was. I suddenly recalled that he wanted to meet up for coffee and talk since he hadn't seen me since the funeral and I had been off work. I picked up my phone and called him.

"Hey, man," I said.

"Where are you?"

Standing up, I walked into the kitchen and looked out the window that faced the ocean. "I'm in Ocean Shores."

"What? When did you guys decide to go there?"

"It's just me, and earlier today."

His tone got serious. "You left Denise at home?"

"Yeah. She didn't want to go." I sat down at the table and began running a finger around the rim of the salt shaker.

"Dude. That's your wife."

"I know."

"You don't make any sense, Micah. You told me you don't just leave your wife."

"I didn't just leave her. She didn't want to come."

"Shouldn't you be at home, taking care of her?"

"I need to take care of myself before I can take care of her. She's hurting and broken, but I'm not doing so well either."

"You okay?"

"No, I'm not okay. My daughter just died!"

"Okay, okay. You're a pretty logical guy, but it just seems . . . illogical."

"I know," I replied softly as I took my finger away from the salt shaker and looked up through the window. "Not a whole lot of my life makes much sense right now."

"Hey. You told me not that long ago that God doesn't think like we do and we're limited in our ability to understand."

"I still have this desire to understand the incomprehensive. It's hard to get past that."

Cole sighed and said, "I can't even imagine what you're going through. Denise, she's okay?"

"She is to a degree. I just got off the phone with her a little bit ago. She sounded better than I've heard in her since this the accident. She still has a lot of pain—we both do—but I think this might be what she needs."

"All right. I'll keep praying for you two. McCormick and I have been praying for you every morning at the station. Alderman even came in one morning and prayed along with us."

"Thank you. Sure was nice that ya'll showed up for the funeral."

"You're one of us. We're there for each other. By the way, the kid's probably getting married in May. I'll let you know when exactly."

I smiled. "I'll be there."

The firemen were like the brothers I never had

growing up. Hanging up with Cole, I headed down the hallway to the bedroom to turn in for the night. It was still early, but I felt exhausted.

CHAPTER 11

Waking up at five the next day, I found myself

unable to get back to sleep. I got out of bed and put
on my gray bathrobe that hung on a hook near the
door that led out to the balcony. Glancing out the
sliding glass door, I saw that it was still dark out.
Opening the door, I took a deep breath of the ocean
air and listened for a moment as the waves crashed
onto the shore in the distance. I smiled as I thought
about how those waves never stopped pushing

against the shoreline and God had put them in motion so long ago.

Closing the door, I journeyed down the stairs and into the kitchen. After realizing I had no fresh coffee in house, I sat down at the kitchen table and grabbed a pen and notepad that were leaning against the napkin holder. I wrote "COFFEE" in big, bold letters at the top and then began wondering what else I needed. Looking over my shoulder into the kitchen, I tried to think, but my Bible sitting on the counter caught my eye. Sighing heavily, I reminded myself I had barely opened it since the accident. That was the real food I needed the most: spiritual. I knew my lack of Bible reading wasn't helping matters in my heart, but I struggled to get myself to read it.

Standing up, I set the pen down and walked over to the counter where the Bible was sitting. Glancing at it, I said, "You're always waiting for me, Lord, aren't you?"

Opening the Bible, it fell open to the book of Job where I had been studying during the weeks up to the accident. Peering up at the ceiling in the kitchen, a smile crept into the corner of my mouth as I realized the parallel between Job and myself. "You sure know how to weave things together. You knew I was going to lose her before I even began this study." Grabbing the worksheet from between the pages, I unfolded it and leaned against the counter as I read my notes. "Oh, Job . . ." I said, shaking my head. "Your suffering was so much greater than mine." Realizing I couldn't read anymore, I placed the paper back into the Bible and closed it.

I grabbed the pen and paper from the table and came around the island. Going through the cupboards in the kitchen, I continued making my list of groceries.

A little later in the morning, the sun began to rise on the horizon and I decided to go for a walk down to the beach. It was only a few minutes to the access point from my back porch. Grabbing my coat off the hook near the back door, I headed outside and down the pathway that led out to the road.

Arriving at the beach, I stopped and admired the golden sunrise coming up over the horizon. The sea went out as far as I could see and the beauty of God was drawn across the sky in yellows and shades of gold. There was no sadness in me as I beheld the glory of God through nature.

"Whatcha looking at, Mister?" a young boy, maybe seven years of age, asked, pulling me from my thoughts.

"Hi, little boy. What's your name?" I asked, bending a knee as I looked behind him, searching for a parent nearby.

"My name's William," he said, extending a hand. I shook his hand and lowered an eyebrow as I looked at him. "Hi, William." I looked around the beach more. "Where are your parents?"

"My parents are in heaven."

"Oh," I said. "Who takes care of you?"

"Charlie."

"And where is he?"

The kid shrugged. "I need to get going, Mister. Have a nice morning." The boy continued walking along the beach away from me. I looked around again and still couldn't spot an adult anywhere nearby. I didn't want to just leave the kid on the beach by himself, so I caught up to his side.

"The sunrise," I said as I caught up to him.

"What?" he asked.

"That's what I was looking at."

The boy looked over at the horizon and said, "Oh. Okay, Mister." The kid kept walking. As I followed next to him, he looked over at me. "Why are you following me?" he asked.

"I need to make sure you get back to your parent."

"You mean Charlie?" he asked.

"Yeah. Charlie. You don't know where he is?"

"He's probably asleep in his chair. Maybe in his office."

"Where do you live?"

"Right on the ocean." The boy pointed down the beach. "Way down there."

"Let's get you home," I said, putting my hand on his shoulder. "Charlie is probably worried about you."

"Charlie doesn't care," the kid replied. His tone didn't seem too bothered by own words.

"Why's that?" I asked as we continued down the beach toward his house.

"I don't know."

We walked for another twenty minutes down the

beach. He told me about his rock collection he'd been working on for a couple years and how he's just about to be done with the second grade. He seemed like a brilliant young man from the small amount of time I spent with him. As we arrived at the wooden steps that led up from the beach to his house, a family with kids walked by. The boy asked, "Do you have any kids, Mister?"

The conversation with William had taken my mind off the accident and everything to do with Jasmine, so when the child presented the question it brought with it all the pain associated with the loss. I cleared my throat and said, "Yeah. One."

"Maybe I can meet them one day," he said, squinting as he looked up at me.

"Maybe," I replied, forcing a smile.

"One more question."

"What?"

"What's your name, Mister?"

"Micah."

He squinted and shook his head. "I'm going to call you Mister."

I laughed. "But why? That's not my name."

"Not everything has a reason." He reached into his coat pocket and pulled out a dark gray rock. To me it looked ordinary and not much different than many of the rocks lying all across the shore. His eyes went wide and he smiled as he kept his eyes locked on it. "This is going to go perfect with the rest."

I smiled as I watched him admire the rock.

"William Lee Johnson!" A man shouted from up the path.

We both looked up to see an angry older gentleman with furrowed eyebrows. He hurried his steps down the path toward us.

I asked the boy, "Is that—"

"Charlie? Yes." The boy shoved the rock back into his pocket and hurried away from me, up the steps toward the man.

"Hello. You must be Charlie. I found—"

"Mind your business, sir!" he said, turning sharply. He glared back at me over his shoulder as he put his arm around William and trekked back up the path. I looked up at beach house they were heading toward. Shingles were coming off the roof, the green paint looked warped and torn, and the back porch of the house didn't look to be in the best condition either. I felt bad for the kid as I turned and walked back down the beach. *Wonder what happened to his parents?* I thought as I glanced back toward the boy's house for a moment. And who was Charlie?

I was walking down an aisle at the grocery store that afternoon when Betty Edmunds, Joe's wife, came around the corner. She made a beeline right for me. Beaming with joy, she stopped her cart next to mine.

"Funny running into you here. How you been?"

"Hi, Betty," I replied. "I'm doing okay."

"I heard about your daughter. I'm so, so sorry. Just heard about it last night, as a matter of fact."

"Okay. Thanks." I tried to push my cart further down the aisle, but she grabbed onto it, stopping it. Looking at her, I said, "Yes, Betty?"

"Look. I know you're hurting, okay? I just know Joe was so happy to see you last night. It'd be good if you spent time with people, you know? People who care about you—and Joe is one of those people."

"I'm sure Joe's busy at the car lot."

"Oh, you didn't hear? He was laid off a couple of weeks back. He's on unemployment now. He has all the time in the world while he waits for callbacks on applications he's turned in. He'd probably love for you to stop by. He's tinkering with his Chevy."

"When did he get a Chevy?" I asked, my interest piqued.

"There's that smile." She laughed. "Anyway. He got it about a month ago. You know, after his dad passed. You didn't hear about that either?"

"I didn't . . . He got the '67 Chevelle, eh?"

"Yep. He didn't mention it at The Home Port? I'm surprised he didn't. He knows how much you love your cars."

"No, he didn't mention it," I replied.

"Stop by the house anytime."

"I might take you up on that offer."

Pushing my cart down the aisle, I thought back to the car show last summer. Joe's Dad had entered his black 1967 Chevelle SS 396 into the car show and walked away with an easy five-hundred-dollar prize for Best in Show. He didn't enter the car shows for the money; he did it for the conversations with the other guys his age that would go to all the same shows up and down the west coast. He was a good man, a deacon in the church and one of the godliest men I had ever met.

After getting all the groceries put away back at the cabin, I went into the living room and called Denise. I told her about Joe's father dying and about running into Betty at the store.

"Oh. I forgot to tell you. I met this kid on the beach this morning."

"A kid?"

"Yeah. He was maybe seven or eight years old. Just walking down the beach at seven o'clock in the morning without a care in the world. No parent or anything."

"Ocean Shores is a bit of a 'keep your doors unlocked' type of a community."

"Yeah, but still. It was strange. He informed me his parents weren't around."

"What do you mean?"

"He said they died. He kept referring to a guy named Charlie as the one who looked after him."

"Did you get him back to the Charlie guy?"

"Yeah. He seemed mean. They live right off the beach."

"Where at on the beach?"

"You know that green house about a mile up from the access point?"

"How am I supposed to remember that?" she asked with a short laugh.

"You know the one. It's broken down and kinda has some overgrowth in the sand dunes in front of it."

"Oh, wait. The one with the big, oddly placed rock in the sand dune?"

"Yep."

She began crying.

My eyes widened. "What?" I asked, leaning forward on the edge of the couch. "What's wrong? Did I say something?"

"No." She sniffed. "It's going to sound weird, but Jasmine danced on that rock two years ago."

Thinking back to the summer she was sixteen, I

recalled the memory. She climbed up the rock and began dancing and singing. She had moments of silliness like that throughout the years. Sighing, I said, "I'm sorry."

"It's okay. I'm just being emotional."

"It's hard. I understand that, Denise. There's no getting around it."

She sniffed again and changed the subject. "Are you going to church tomorrow?"

"I don't know," I replied. Looking over at my Bible sitting on the counter, I said, "I know I need to."

"Me too . . . I get sick of people talking to me about the accident, though."

"It gets old."

"Megan stopped by today. She brought me a gift basket of bath oils and stuff as a gift from her and Cole."

"That was sweet of them," I replied, knowing that Cole was trying to look out for Denise and make sure she was doing okay. He had my back no matter what the situation was.

"She said she wanted to check in and make sure everything was okay. Made me feel good to be thought of."

I smiled. "It's those little things that really touch the heart. Isn't it?"

"It sure is." "Hey, Micah . . ."

"Yeah?"

"We're going to be okay someday, right?"

"Yeah. We're going to be okay."

CHAPTER 12

On the following morning I headed down to the

beach to watch the sunrise. I was also a bit curious if
I'd see the boy out traversing the sandy beach again.
Sure enough, he was. I walked across the sand and
up to him. "Good morning, William."

"Mister," he said as he turned and continued
walking past me down the beach. I noticed a bruise
on his cheek.

Grabbing his shoulder, I stopped him and said,
"How'd that bruise get on you?"

He cupped his face and said softly, "I fell." He shrugged my hand off him and kept going. I followed along with him down the shoreline.

"Is that what really happened?"

He didn't respond. Instead he just kept walking.

"Did that Charlie guy hurt you?" I asked.

He stopped and looked up at me. "No. Why do you care so much?"

"If he hit you?" Glancing up the beach toward his house, I continued, "I don't think any child should be harmed. It's not right."

He dipped his chin to his chest and continued walking without a word. I decided not to follow him this time; instead I stayed back and just let him walk alone. Taking a seat in the sand, I watched as William walked up and down the beach. He'd stop every few steps to pick up some random rock that caught his eye and then continue on. He went far enough down the beach that I couldn't even see him. Then he turned back and began working his way up the shore again.

As he stopped near me to pick up a rock, I asked, "Could I see the rocks?"

He came over to me and emptied his pockets out in the sand in front of me. A random collection of grays, blacks and even a few pieces of driftwood made it into the assortment.

"Why do you collect them?" I asked.

He shrugged as he looked down at the rocks and sat crisscrossed across from me. "I like how God made them all different. He made them unique. Like me."

"Wow. That's pretty profound for a seven-year-old."

"I'm not seven. I'm eight and a half." He glanced down toward the direction of his house. "I better go home."

Standing up, I said, "I'll walk you."

"No!" he demanded, pushing out a hand as he scooped up the rocks with his other.

"All right. All right. You sure you're okay?"

"Yeah. I'm fine." After making sure his rocks were all securely in his pockets, he ventured down the beach. I watched him as he walked and wondered what this little boy's story was. Who was Charlie, and was he lying about the bruise not being from him?

Later that day, after lunch, I drove to Joe's place that was a few houses up from mine. There was a chilly wind in the air, so driving made more sense. When I pulled into the driveway I could see Joe working on the Chevelle just inside the open garage. Parking, I got out and smiled as I approached the garage and took in the view of the classic piece of American history. The black paint was immaculate and I could hardly believe there was an issue with the car that he would have to be fixing.

"Hey, Joe," I said, coming up to his feet that were sticking out from underneath the front of the car. He slid out from underneath the car and smiled as he wiped his hand off with the dirty towel he had tucked in his jean pocket. He extended his hand to me, and I grabbed it and helped him up to his feet. "How's it going?"

"I'm okay. Betty told me about your Dad. Sorry to hear that."

He looked down for a moment and nodded. "Circle of life, ya know?"

"Yep."

He turned and looked at the car. "Got the car. Was pretty stoked about it until I discovered some hose leaks. But at least that's minor."

"That's not too bad," I replied as I looked the car over. "You going to continue on the legacy and take it to the car shows this summer?"

"Oh, yeah," he replied as looked at the car. He let his fingers glide across the smooth exterior of the car as he began to walk around it. Pausing at the passenger side door, he looked over at me. "Loss is hard."

"Yeah, it is," I replied. I could see Joe's hurt in his eyes. He was going through something similar to me and I felt obligated to say something about Jasmine. "I lost Jasmine a few weeks ago."

His eyes went wide. "What?"

I looked down and fixated my eyes on an oil stain on the smooth cement floor. Keeping my eyes locked on it, I said, "Car accident."

Joe came around the car and to me. "I'm so sorry, man. I wouldn't have been that way at The Home Port if I had any idea."

"It's okay," I replied as tears welled in my eyes. Joe shook his head.

"That is a parent's worst nightmare. I'm sorry you had to go through it."

"It'll be all right."

"Does Pastor Clarkson know?"

"Yeah. He probably saw the status update I sent out."

He nodded. "I'm a little out of the loop with how much I'm disconnected."

"Yeah, but you're doing it for the right reasons. You don't need to be bombarded by all the drama of the world on there."

"Yeah. Thankfully the wife agrees with my choice and doesn't tell me things she learns. She struggled at first, but she's been doing pretty well. It can be hard at times, like this, for instance, but truly I have been relying on God more than ever after losing the job at the dealership."

"You looking for work?"

He shrugged. "Here and there; I'm picking up side jobs." Glancing at the car, he said, "Worst case scenario is I don't take the car to the shows this summer and I sell this baby."

"You can't sell that, man. It was your Dad's car."

"I need to take care of my family more than anything. I'll have Betty snap a picture of me and it and sell it if it comes down to it. I'm not going to let my family struggle so I can keep a hunk of metal."

My eyebrows went up.

"Sorry, I know how much cars mean to you."

"No, no. I'm intrigued."

"It's more than just using the money to pay bills. Medical debt from the kids and wife are stacking up. That was true even when we had medical through the dealership." He let out a heavy sigh and shook his head. Looking at me, he smiled and said, "But God's good and I'm thankful. It's just a car that I can't take to heaven when all is said and done."

I nodded. "That's true."

"By the way, we missed you at Church this morning. I was hoping you'd be there."

"Yeah. I didn't go," I replied with a sharp tone.

He paused and looked at me for a moment. I made eye contact with him, and he narrowed his gaze at me. "You have a beef with God?"

I furrowed my eyebrows at him. "That's between God and me."

"I'll keep praying for you. The pain in this life doesn't define who we are; God does."

"I know. Just hard at moments."

"I understand."

Joe and I finished checking hoses and replaced the ones that we could find that were damaged. He wasn't as obnoxious as I remembered him from the other visits I'd had to Ocean Shores. It was nice spending time with the guy. Once we were done a few hours later, my stomach was growling.

"I'd better get home and eat."

"Join us for dinner," he offered. "Betty's making a ham and there's plenty of food."

"I couldn't impose," I replied, raising a hand.

"I insist. You helped me out today with the car. Just join us for a meal."

"All right," I replied with a smile.

We walked up the cement path to the house. We went inside and took off our coats, hanging them on the coat rack near the door. The smell of ham filled the air inside as I took a seat on the couch in the living room.

"You joining us for dinner?" Betty asked, walking in

from the kitchen.

"Yep. Your husband extended an offer I couldn't refuse."

Joe laughed. "I didn't give him much of an option."

"Good!" Betty said, smiling. "Take a seat in the dining room. Dinner is ready; I just need to get the kids."

Going into the dining room, I smiled as I looked out the giant bay window that overlooked the ocean down below. They had a marvelous beachfront view, which was closer to the ocean than my cabin, even though we were only a few houses apart. I could see right down onto the beach and could even see the seagulls landing and taking off.

Sitting down, I unfolded the napkin that was on a plate in front of me and set it in my lap as the family joined me at the table. Betty brought in the pot of mashed potatoes, corn and a basket of rolls while Joe brought in the sliced ham on a serving platter. It all looked amazing.

Joe blessed the food and everyone began eating. Not long into the meal I spotted someone down on the beach out of the corner of my eye. It was a child.

Wondering if it was William, I stood up and set my napkin down on the table next to my plate. Going over to the window, I squinted and looked.

"What do you see? An ocean?" Joe asked with a chuckle.

I smiled and replied, "I'm seeing if that kid is the same one I've been seeing on the beach the last couple of mornings."

"You've been meeting a kid on the beach?" Betty asked.

I saw the kid bend down and grab something from the sand.

"It's him," I said, going for the sliding door.

"What are you doing?" Joe asked.

"I'm going to go see how he is. I'll be back."

Going out the back door, I hurried down the wooden steps that led all the way down to the beach.

I ran up to him and he stopped and looked at me. He was bundled up tightly in a jacket with a scarf and a beanie this time. Muffled, he said, "Hi, Mister."

"What are you doing out here? It's freezing and

going to get dark soon. You were looking for rocks again?" I asked, wrapping my arms around myself to keep my warmth.

He shook his head. "I did find one. But I mostly just came to walk the beach. Do some thinking."

"You're eight years old. What do you have to think about?"

He didn't reply, just looked at the sand he was kicking between his sneakers. "Sometimes I think about my parents."

"You remember them?" I asked.

"A little."

"How long ago did they . . ."

"Die? Few years ago."

Glancing back up at Joe's house, I could see him and Betty staring down at us. Turning my attention back to William, I asked, "Have you eaten dinner yet?"

"No."

"You want to come meet some friends of mine? There is plenty of food to eat and it's warm inside."

"Okay."

We walked up the shore and went up the steps back up to Joe's house. As we got up to the door, I said,

"I'll drive you home in a bit. After we eat."

He undid his scarf and revealed a smile. "Thanks, Mister."

"You're welcome," I replied, returning a smile as I opened the door.

"Hello there, William," Betty said, bending at the knees to meet William eye level. "Would you like some ham?"

"You know him?" I asked.

"He goes to our church. You would have known that if you came today," Joe said with a smile.

William nodded and smiled at Betty. "That'd be great, Mrs. Edmunds."

"Such a sweet boy," Betty said, rising to her feet and heading into the kitchen.

Sitting down at the table next to Lonnie, William looked over at him and said, "hi."

Lonnie was fourteen and smiled at him. "Hey."

"You're Charlie Prescott's young'un, right?"

He nodded.

Betty came in from the kitchen and set a plate down with silverware in front of William while I took my seat back at the dining table next to Joe.

"What's your favorite thing about the beach?" Joe asked.

"I'm guessing the rocks," I said.

"Let the kid answer," Joe laughed.

"God," William said.

Everyone stopped eating and looked over at the kid. Joe set his fork down and wiped his mouth with his napkin. "God?"

"Yeah," the kid replied.

"What about Him?" Joe asked, leaning in as he rested his chin on his hand.

"He knows how many pieces of sand are on that beach. He made the fish in the ocean and created everything you can see."

"He did," Joe said, nodding as he smiled. "Your grandpa must be doing a swell job with you."

William ignored the comment and looked toward the window as the sun was setting. "It's comforting to know how big God is, and that beach reminds me of it every day."

Everyone's eyes widened at the dinner table. Who was this kid? I wondered. If only I could capture his relentless faith.

"Out of the mouths of babes comes wisdom!" Joe said with a clap. "Wow!" He said as he picked up his fork and took another bite of his ham. Shaking his fork at William as he finished his bite, he said, "Your faith is inspiring!"

"Thanks," William replied as he grabbed a roll and a few slabs of ham off the plate in the middle of the table. He looked so happy to be around these people. I felt like I did the right thing bringing him inside from the shore.

CHAPTER 13

After an enjoyable meal and a visit with the

Edmunds it was time to take William home. Getting into the truck and firing it up, I let the engine warm up and rubbed my hands together to gather warmth. Sounds of sniffling came from William in the passenger seat.

"What's wrong?" I asked. "Didn't you have a good time with the Edmunds?"

"It's not that," he replied, wiping his eyes.

"What is it?" I asked, putting the truck into drive. We began down the street toward his house.

"Charlie's going to be mad . . ." he said as we came up to his house.

Slowing down as I pulled over to the curb in front of his house, I asked, "Why?"

"I was gone a long time," William replied. A kid out on his own wasn't okay, but this Charlie guy seemed to be rather uninvolved, and if he was hitting the kid, it made sense why he didn't want to be around the house.

Putting the truck in park, I turned to him.

"William."

He looked over at me for a second before turning his head back to the floor of the truck. He began sobbing again. "William," I said again.

He looked at me with his big brown eyes and asked, "What?"

"I'm going to ask you something and I need you to be honest."

"Okay."

"Does Charlie hit you?"

He shook his head and looked out the window

toward his house. "If I say anything they'll take me away and I'll be all alone."

"Who will? What are you talking about?"

He began crying uncontrollably.

Placing a hand on his shoulder, I said, "What's wrong? You can talk to me."

"He does hit me! Okay?" William lashed out. "But the mean people with coats will take me away and make me live with someone I don't know if they find out. I don't want them to take me!" He began crying into his hands. "I don't want to be alone."

My anger kindled inside of me as I looked over at the house. I didn't agree with William walking around on the beach alone, but no child ever deserved to be beaten. "I'm going to talk to Charlie."

"No!" he pleaded as he looked me. "Please don't talk to him! He'll hit me more."

"Let me walk you up to the door."

"No!" he shouted and jumped out of the truck, slamming the door behind him. Slipping slightly on the ice on his way up the sidewalk, he caught himself and continued up to the door and went inside.

I was torn on what to do. Going to the Lord in prayer, I began praying for Charlie and William. I prayed He would protect William from harm. Then suddenly I heard a crash come from inside the house. Stopping my prayer, I looked over. I couldn't see anything, but I heard another crash inside. Then the light went out that was previously shining through the curtains in the front of the house. "What is going on in there?" I asked out loud to myself, getting out of the truck. Adrenaline began coursing through me as my heart began to race and I approached the house. There was no way I was going to willingly drive away knowing that man was mostly likely hurting that boy. Walking up to the house, I tried to see through the curtains but it was dark. A back door swung open and I heard William crying from behind the house. Running, I rounded the corner of the house just as Charlie raised a belt above his head and William lay shaking on the deck. "Hey!" I shouted.

Charlie turned to me and lowered his hands down to his sides. He glared toward me and said through his teeth, "Why don't you mind your own business?"

"I'm not going to let you hurt that child."

Charlie laughed and came to the edge of the deck where a set of stairs sat. Looking down at me with a worn smile, he asked, "How you plan to do that? You're on my property."

My jaw clenched as I took a step forward, closer to the steps that led up to him. He took a step down and began wrapping the belt around his balled fist. "After I get done with you, I'm going to give Willy a lesson in manne—"

I lost all control over myself and lunged toward him. He moved over and I missed, sending myself face first into the deck.

As I pushed myself off the deck to get up, I heard the sound of a gun clicking behind me. "Get off my property!" Charlie shouted as I stood up.

I turned around and he circled around me with the gun pointed at my face. Glancing over at William, he said, "Get inside, boy!"

William scrambled up from the deck and ran into the house through the back door.

"I don't want any trouble," I said as my eyes fixated on the barrel that was pointed my way.

"You better get off my property in the next five seconds, or I'll put a bullet between your eyes."

I inched myself backward and off the deck, hands up in the air. My heart was pounding as I watched Charlie go inside and I could hear the deadbolt on the door lock. Hurrying back around the house and out to my truck, I could hear screams coming from inside the house, causing the knot in my chest to turn.

Getting into my truck, I clenched my jaw as I looked over at the house. My eyes fell on the address –7554. Turning the key over, I began driving. Phoning the police, I explained to the woman at dispatch what had happened.

"Can you have the officer who goes over there to call me afterwards?" I asked as I pulled into my driveway.

"Sure," the woman replied.

"Thank you." Breathing a sigh of relief, I hung up and looked out my passenger side window to spot Joe taking the trash out to the curb. I wondered if he knew anything about Charlie beating on William. Getting out of my truck, I jogged down the sidewalk and caught Joe before he made it back into his house.

"Hey, Joe!" I shouted as I paused to catch my breath in his driveway.

"Hey," he replied, coming back off his porch.

Walking over to me, he asked, "Are you okay?"

Shaking my head as I stood upright, I said, "No."

"What's wrong?"

"It's William. Listen—do you know Charlie?"

"Charlie Prescott? Well, yeah. He's one of the deacons at Christ Community. Why?"

"I'm pretty confident he's beating William."

Joe's composure shifted immediately as he adjusted his footing and furrowed his eyebrows. "You're mistaken."

"No. I was just over there and—"

"I said you're mistaken."

"Why are you—" My phone buzzed in my pocket, it was an unknown local number. I assumed it was the police. Holding a finger up to Joe for a moment, I turned and answered it.

"Is this the gentleman that called in a report on a possible child abuse issue?"

"Yep. Did you go over there and get Charlie?"

"What's your address, Mr. Freeman?"

"616 Canal Dr."

"I'll be over in a few minutes to talk to you."

Click.

Turning back around to Joe, he looked upset.

"You'd better not go accusing a deacon of child abuse, Micah. Or you're going to have some wrath coming."

"I don't care if he is a deacon. If there is foul play, he needs to be brought to justice."

"I've known Mr. Prescott for many, many years. He'd never lay a hand on a child in a non-Biblical disciplinary way. He probably just spanked him." Joe took a step closer to me. "And there ain't anything wrong with spankings."

I raised my hands and took a step back. "I agree with spanking children." Looking back toward my house, I knew I needed to get back. "A policeman is coming over to my house. I need to get back home."

"Okay. Don't chase an idea because you *think* you know something. You don't want to hurt a brother in Christ."

"I'm not trying to hurt anyone. I'm trying to protect the child."

"Just be careful, that's all I'm trying to say." Joe went inside his house and slammed the door behind him.

Why was Joe so protective of Charlie? *Maybe the history they had between them*, I thought to myself as I walked down the sidewalk and back toward the house. Getting halfway up my driveway, the police cruiser showed up.

"Good evening, Officer," I said with a nod as he stepped out of his car.

"Evening," he replied. Stepping onto the sidewalk, he looked over at my house.

"Let's go inside and talk," I said.

He agreed with a nod and we went inside and sat down in the living room. As the officer got comfortable on the couch, I offered him a drink. "I have coffee, water or juice."

"No, thank you."

"Okay," I replied and came and sat down next to the officer on the couch.

"Your story here says you went to drop off the eight-year-old boy named William and when you were about to leave the curb of the house, you heard shouting and a light went off inside. You went to investigate and saw Charlie about to beat William with a belt, but you interrupted it by dashing over to him and trying to tackle Charlie."

"Yes."

"Okay. And then he threatened you with a gun?"

"Yep."

"Well, I collected a different story from Mr. Prescott and William."

"You saw William?" I asked, leaning in. "Was he okay?"

"He had a bruise on his eye he got from falling down and hitting an end table. Then a large gash that looked fairly recent, but William even said he was just being clumsy."

"He's lying!" I shouted, jumping to my feet. "Both of them. Don't you get it? The kid is scared he'll be taken away."

The officer's eyebrows furrowed as he rose to his feet. "We'll keep investigating, but you should leave this investigation work to us." He turned and headed for the door.

I walked with him and opened the door.

"Give me a call if you see anything that you're worried about," the officer said, handing me a business card.

"Thanks," I replied, shutting the door.

CHAPTER 14

After a sleepless night, I woke up and headed out to beach right away so I could speak with William about what had happened last night. I wanted to see if he was okay. The chilly April morning wind was gusting as I walked the sandy coastline that morning. Traveling up and down the beach several times, I couldn't see William. My worry began to soar as I made my way to the portion of the beach just outside their property.

Looking up toward the green house beyond the sand dunes and tall grass, I tried to see through the windows that were facing the ocean side, but I couldn't see anything.

Where was William? Did Charlie not let him come out to walk this morning? The thoughts circled my mind as I walked back toward the entrance to the beach I had come down through.

Getting back up to my house, I sat down at the kitchen table and began to pray.

Help me, Lord, I don't know what to do. Please protect William.

My phone rang, interrupting my prayer. It was Denise.

"Hello?"

"Hey," she said. "You okay? I didn't hear from you last night."

"Got some drama going on. That kid I met on the beach is getting beaten, I'm pretty sure."

"How'd that end up being your issue? I'm sorry if that sounded rude. I'm just confused."

My eyebrows furrowed as I felt almost offended by the comment. "What do you mean? He's the kid I met on the beach the other day that I told you about. If he's being abused, then he needs out of the situation, Denise."

She began crying.

"I'm sorry. I didn't mean to upset you. I'm just worried about him."

"No . . . It's good you're trying to protect him and watch out for the kid."

"Then what's wrong?"

She sniffled and took a deep breath. "I'm just sitting in this empty house alone and can't stop thinking about Jasmine. Sure, I'm feeling better, but I still have my moments . . ."

Suddenly, like an ocean wave crashing up on the shore, all the grief and pain with the loss of Jasmine came rushing back over me. I had been so distracted by this boy and his problems that I had almost forgotten about Jasmine. I felt guilty and ashamed.

"I'm sorry," I said in a soft tone.

Then she asked a question that jarred me and forced me to think. "You sure you aren't just chasing this boy and his problems to avoid your own?"

"I hadn't thought of that." Was I doing that? Was I

fixating on this kid to help avoid my own emotional turmoil over the loss of my daughter? I wasn't entirely sure, but it sounded likely.

"Just be careful. You could mess up lives by injecting yourself where you don't belong. And some day this drama will be over and you'll still have to deal with the loss of Jasmine, if you are in fact avoiding it by keeping distracted by the boy."

My lips pressed together to form a thin line at the realization she was right. My wife was truly my help mate for life. She sharpened me and helped me be the man of God I needed to be. If it wasn't for her continuous help, I wouldn't be the man of God I had become over the years. She had an ability to shine light on an issue I didn't even see.

Relaxing and taking a deep breath, I said, "Thank you, Denise."

"Get in your Bible. You're there to get right with God, not right the wrongs in the world."

"You're right." Standing up from the table, I walked over to the couch in the living room and sat down. "How you holding up over there?"

"Pretty good. I found a grief support group with one

of the neighboring churches. Pam Aldridge is the leader."

"Oh, I remember her. She ran that Christmas Dinner a few years back."

"Yeah. She met with me yesterday for lunch and we had a good cry."

"She lost a kid?"

"Mmhmm . . . It was about twelve years ago. She lost her four-year-old boy. He ran into oncoming traffic just outside a restaurant and was hit by a truck."

"That is terrible . . ."

"Yeah. She said she was messed up for a long time. She pointed out that I could still have hope-filled joy because of God, and cautioned me that happiness depends on your circumstances; joy depends on God and my relationship with Him. She told me a lot of helpful things about how to deal with my new life and I felt for the first time like someone understood me."

"I'm happy you are finding relief and help."

"It's a long journey, but I can tell I'm already beginning to feel better."

"Good," I replied. Knowing my wife was on the right

path brought me comfort. Looking over to the kitchen, I saw the Bible sitting on the counter. "I'm going to dive into some scripture."

I could hear a smile on the other end of the line. "Good. I'll let you go do that."

Hanging up, I headed over to the kitchen and grabbed my Bible. Returning to the living room, I sat down and opened the Scriptures. I went straight to reading the next chapter of Job.

Job 28

There is a mine for silver
and a place where gold is refined.
2 Iron is taken from the earth,
and copper is smelted from ore.
3 Mortals put an end to the darkness;
they search out the farthest recesses
for ore in the blackest darkness.
4 Far from human dwellings they cut a shaft,
in places untouched by human feet;
far from other people they dangle and sway.
5 The earth, from which food comes,
is transformed below as by fire;

6 lapis lazuli comes from its rocks,

and its dust contains nuggets of gold.

7 No bird of prey knows that hidden path,

no falcon's eye has seen it.

8 Proud beasts do not set foot on it,

and no lion prowls there.

9 People assault the flinty rock with their hands

and lay bare the roots of the mountains.

10 They tunnel through the rock;

their eyes see all its treasures.

11 They search the sources of the rivers

and bring hidden things to light.

12 But where can wisdom be found?

Where does understanding dwell?

13 No mortal comprehends its worth;

it cannot be found in the land of the living.

14 The deep says, "It is not in me";

the sea says, "It is not with me."

15 It cannot be bought with the finest gold,

nor can its price be weighed out in silver.

16 It cannot be bought with the gold of Ophir,

with precious onyx or lapis lazuli.

17 Neither gold nor crystal can compare with it, nor

can it be had for jewels of gold.
18 Coral and jasper are not worthy of mention;
the price of wisdom is beyond rubies.
19 The topaz of Cush cannot compare with it;
it cannot be bought with pure gold.
20 Where then does wisdom come from?
Where does understanding dwell?
21 It is hidden from the eyes of every living thing,
concealed even from the birds in the sky.
22 Destruction and Death say,
"Only a rumor of it has reached our ears."
23 God understands the way to it
and he alone knows where it dwells,
24 for he views the ends of the earth
and sees everything under the heavens.
25 When he established the force of the wind
and measured out the waters,
26 when he made a decree for the rain
and a path for the thunderstorm,
27 then he looked at wisdom and appraised it;
he confirmed it and tested it.
28 And he said to the human race,
"The fear of the Lord—that is wisdom,

and to shun evil is understanding."

Bowing my head, I prayed for God to write the verses on my heart and to infuse my being with the Scriptures, especially with the last few verses, which outlined God's power and strength. The Lord decreed the rain and set the path for the thunderstorms, yet I had the nerve to question His plan? I had no right.

Then a realization of the truth came to me as I prayed.

That inner voice that kept telling me I couldn't do it before was correct all along. I couldn't do anything. It was God, who lived within me, that could do it. I wasn't part of the equation, only a vessel for the solution. My eyes filled with tears as I dropped my chin to my chest and slid off the couch and onto my knees. Crying out as I brought my hands together on the coffee table in front of me, I said, "God, please forgive me. I was trying to do this all on my own, without realizing YOU are the only one that can do it. It's through Your power alone that my heart can be healed. I might never fully understand why

Jasmine had to die, but I know You have a plan for good and that Jasmine is with You now. Help me to rely on You alone. Amen."

A knock on my back door startled me slightly. *Who could that be?* I wondered, standing up. I wiped my eyes and cheeks and then headed over to the door. Opening it, I saw it was little William. With a gash across his head and tears running down his cheeks, he asked, "Mister. Could I come in?"

"Sure, William," I said opening the door fully to let him inside. He came inside and we went into the living room. Sitting down on the couch, I said, "What's going on?"

He sniffled and began crying. "Charlie . . ."

"Yeah? What happened?" I asked, placing a hand on his shoulder.

"You made him nervous. He's really mad now and said if he catches me hanging out with you again he'll send me away forever."

"I see," I replied.

William's eyes fell onto the open Bible and a smile shone through his tears. "Whatcha reading about?" he asked, being entirely drawn to the Bible and out of his sadness.

"Job. He's talking about wisdom."

William got down on his knees and began to read the passage out loud.

"Don't you have to get back home?"

"Charlie went to the church for a bit. He'll be gone for at least an hour." Turning his attention back to the Scriptures, he continued to read the chapter, sounding each word out when he got stuck. When he finished, he said, "See, Micah?"

"What?" I asked, leaning over his shoulder to look.

"It's right here, Micah. God's so big and wonderful and amazing. He's doing something in our lives. Each one of us. We have to trust that."

"You sure seem wise for a kid," I replied with a raised eyebrow.

"According to Job, wisdom is the fear of the Lord and shunning evil. There isn't an age requirement on wisdom." He glanced toward the back door as he continued. "Since my parents died I've spent a lot of time reading the Bible and trying to understand why my parents died. I felt like God took them from me and left me with my mean old grandpa. But I've realized through promises like in Jeremiah that God has a plan for our lives. God knew I was going to meet you on the beach that day. He knew we'd be sitting here right now. He's in control more than we sometimes think."

I nodded. "You're right."

"I need you to do something for me," he said, looking at me with those big, brown eyes. "I need you to stay away from me. I don't want to upset Charlie again and I need to stay there."

"Okay. But why won't you tell the cops the truth?"

He shook his head. "If I do, they'll take me away and my brother might never find me."

"Your brother? Where's he at?"

"I don't know . . . he was older when my parents died. He wasn't living at home at the time. I lost contact with him after Charlie moved into our house. If I leave Charlie's, he'd never find me."

My heart broke into pieces at the hope I could sense in William's voice and see through his eyes. He was waiting for his brother to come back. "Do you ask your grandpa about him?"

He nodded. "I have, but he just says he died. I don't

believe him, though. I think he just tells me that so I don't talk about it." He looked over at the clock on the wall near the hallway. "I better get back."

"All right," I said, standing up with him. We walked over to the door and I looked outside as I opened the door for him. Seeing the ocean in the distance, I said, "Don't give up hope, William."

He smiled and I closed the door. I watched as William walked down the steps and onto the path that led to the road back to the beach. Curious what the deal was with his brother, I went back into the living room and called Joe.

"What happened to William's parents?"

"Why you asking about that?"

"I'm curious."

"They died. Not much else to know."

"Okay. Do you know what happened to their other son?"

"Blake vanished after the night of the accident. His girlfriend at the time said he left town on a bus and she never saw him again."

"Who was his girlfriend?"

"Jessica Sanders." Joe cleared his throat. "Charlie's

the only family that boy has. It's best if you don't poke your nose where it doesn't belong or he might even lose him."

I hung up on him. I didn't need the manipulation I was sensing from his end of the phone. Bowing my head, I prayed for God to help me understand what I'm supposed to do.

I don't know if you want me to pursue this boy's freedom or if I need to be focused on You alone, Lord. A voice from within my soul whispered into my thoughts, *Why not both?*

Thank you, Lord. Help me walk in the light and the Spirit and not in selfishness. Amen.

I had peace flowing through me as I lifted my head. Pursuing a solution for William was something I needed to do.

After dinner, I phoned Denise to update her on what happened with William coming over and the decision I'd made to pursue helping the boy. She listened quietly until the end.

"If you help this boy, you'd better be praying every step of the way, Micah Freeman. You must also be aware of the consequences."

"No need to sound like my mother," I replied curtly.

"Hey, now. I'm far from being your mother, but I am your wife, Micah! It's my duty to be your help mate. I'm trying to help."

She was right. "I'm sorry. Thank you. I'm just nervous."

"You should be. I called Betty after our phone call earlier to see what the deal was with this Charlie guy. She informed me that Charlie Prescott is not only a deacon in the church, but a member of the city council and a highly regarded figure in the community."

"Hmm."

"It's serious, Micah. Betty even said he has ties with the chief of police in town and the judges. You'd better tread lightly with whatever you do moving forward."

"If God is for us, who can stand against us?"

"Romans 8:31," she replied. I could hear the smile in her voice on the other end of the phone.

"Exactly." Looking over at a family picture of her, myself and Jasmine that sat on the entertainment center, I said, "God's up to something with all of this. I can feel it."

"He is always working on something, isn't he?" she said. "It makes me so happy that you're getting back in your Bible. I can hear it in your voice."

"I feel better. I was doing my study in Job today. Job 28 and how wisdom was put into place, just like when God measured the waters and set the path of thunderstorms into place. It makes me think about how small of an existence we truly have on this earth. We are like a speck of sand on the beach, and yet we sometimes get hung up on our own speck so much that we forget how we ended up on the beach to begin with. Our Creator put us there."

"Mmm . . ." Denise replied. "Keep talking."

"What?"

"Your voice. It's comforting."

I smiled and continued on. We cried, we laughed, we talked for over an hour about a lot of different things. We both figured out we weren't really sure how to proceed after our daughter passed away, but we knew God was with us. Our talk even touched on the possibility of going to the Congo for a missionary trip later the next year. And as the night's talk was wrapping up, Denise asked a question I'd never forget.

"How do Christians as devoted as we are sometimes lose perspective of who God is?"

It was such a deep and yet simple question. It challenged me to my core. It forced me reflect inwardly and analyze my actions following the death of our daughter. I replied, "Even the best of us lose perspective at moments of weakness. The enemy exploits those weaknesses and if we don't have God's strength to hold us up in that area, we fail."

"I love you," she said. "That's such a good way to look at it. Hey, you know what just came to mind?"

"What?"

"I think the passage that tells us to keep our minds renewed daily parallels what you just said."

"Corinthians 4:16: 'Therefore we do not lose heart. Though outwardly we are wasting away, yet inwardly we are being renewed day by day.' It does go well with it, but it goes deeper. I've been praying and reading my Bible every single day, yet even though I was renewed, I failed."

"I disagree. You came out of it. You were renewed. You didn't fail," Denise retorted.

"True, but I did fail. You weren't inside my mind, honey. I wasn't very happy with God and what happened to our baby girl."

"How?" she asked.

"I think my weakness with our daughter was the fact that I thought she was mine to begin with. She was the Lord's all along. He knew when I held my baby girl in my hands the day she was born that she would die in that car accident, on that day and at that exact time."

Denise began crying. "Stop."

I relaxed my neck into the back of the couch and looked up at the ceiling. "God's in control, and while I have always believed that, I failed in trusting Him for a bit after losing Jasmine. Remember when Cole and Megan went through all that stuff in their marriage?"

"Yeah."

"I told him that he needs to funnel everything in life

through God first. I failed to do that with our daughter."

"I think you're being a bit harsh with yourself, Micah."

"I don't think so, Denise. God is above all. Not above *some*, but all!"

"Okay," Denise replied. "I'm going to do some reading and turn in for the evening. I enjoyed talking to you."

"It's been a while since we talked." I smiled. "I enjoyed it too."

Hanging up with Denise, I thought about God and how He was in control of everything. God's insight to the world around me was far greater than even a sliver of my understanding.

I wasn't ready to turn in for the evening yet, so I phoned the Chief to see how he was doing.

"How are you?" I asked.

"Still recovering. I feel like an idiot hugging this teddy bear every time I need to cough."

I laughed. "It helps the pain, I'm sure."

"It does. It does. Heard you took off to Ocean Shores?"

"Yeah. Needed some time to get away."

"I see. I'm glad you called. I wanted to tell you something. When I was counting down backward as I went under, I focused on one word that you said to me in that conversation earlier."

"And what's that?"

"Hope."

I smiled.

"I just wanted to pass that along to you. After all that's happened . . . I felt like I should share that with you. Your being there for me meant a lot. And I'm truly sorry about Jasmine."

"Thank you," I replied. "Hope is what we have as Christians. Someday down the line I will see my daughter again in Heaven, and that does bring me comfort. That hope brings me unspeakable peace."

We chatted for a while longer about how the recovery was going for him and how the guys were suspicious about his extended vacation since he hadn't missed more than a few days of work in all the time he had worked there. He told me he was going to say something, but he just wanted to wait for the perfect time to do so—maybe get a bit more healed up before breaking the news to the guys. I think he was just scared to admit that he wasn't the man of steel that everybody at the station thought he was.

CHAPTER 15

My investigation was in full swing the next

morning. The first stop was the Community church
to see if Pastor Clarkson could shed any light on the
situation with Charlie and William. Getting out of
my truck in the parking lot, I headed up to the doors
of the church. I tried to pull it open, but found it
surprisingly locked.

That's strange, I thought to myself as I looked
through the glass doors. Seeing the Pastor's office

door open, I saw someone look out at me and then shut the door. What's that about? *Maybe they didn't see me*, I thought, giving the door a few firm knocks. The gentleman came out and over to the door. Unlocking it, he pushed it open and stepped to the side to let me in. "Sorry about that. We were just having a little business meeting."

"It's all right," I replied, stepping inside.

The gentleman continued out to the parking lot and I went to the pastor's office. Knocking on the door gently as I pushed it open, I smiled as my eyes fell on Pastor Clarkson.

He looked up at me and returned the smile. "Micah," he said, standing up and extending a hand to shake mine.

We shook hands and sat down.

"What brings you by so early? It's barely past eight in the morning."

I nodded. "It's William."

"Hmm . . ." he replied. His attitude shifted dramatically as he leaned back in his seat and crossed his arms. "What about him? Was he breaking windows with those darn rocks again?"

"What? No."

Pastor Clarkson dropped his hands down to the desk as he leaned in and lowered his voice. "That boy is trouble. We caught him breaking windows at Mrs. Ellis's house back a few months ago." The pastor shook his head and leaned back in his chair. "Kid has been trouble ever since his parents passed a few years back." He looked at me with narrowed eyes. "What'd he do?"

"It's not what he did."

The pastor raised an eyebrow. "Oh?"

"I'm trying to find his brother."

He shook his head. "Blake skipped town the night their parents died and nobody has seen or heard from him since. There are a few rumors floating around town that he's the one that killed the parents."

"Caused the car accident?"

He nodded. "Yeah. And now he's gone. Was there anything else I could do for you?"

"Yeah. There's one more thing. Could you tell me where Jessica Sanders might be?"

The pastor tipped his chin and then gave me a hard

look. "Don't know."

"She stopped coming to church?"

"Yep." Leaning back in across the desk, he asked, "What's this all about? Why are you trying to figure out any of this?"

"I'm just worried about William."

"Why? Charlie's been a blessing for that boy since his momma and father passed onto glory. He moved into their house and has been providing a life for William ever since."

"I'm just worried that Charlie might be hurting him."

"Charlie Prescott hurting him? I can guarantee you that the only hurt that boy is feeling is on his backside for misbehaving! But I'll look into it," he replied. "I did notice a bruise on him the other day."

"Yeah. So you saw that?" I asked.

"Sure did. I'll talk to Charlie. We go way back."

"No," I said. "Please don't. I'm afraid it'll cause more issues for William than it would solve."

"Okay. I'll ask around elsewhere. You don't worry about it anymore. I will take it from here, son."

"All right." I stood up and shook his hand. "Thanks for all the help, Pastor."

"It's my pleasure," he replied, smiling. "How's everything else going?"

"I'm fine," I replied. "Thanks."

After lunch, I went over to a gas station to fill up. While waiting in line to pay for my gas, I overheard the guy in front of me talking to the man behind the counter.

"Jessica's not going to the party tonight. She said she's sick of that whole scene."

Could that be Jessica Sanders? I wondered. The pastor was pretty curt about the topic of Jessica Sanders; it wouldn't hurt to at least ask the gentlemen in front of me.

"When you gonna drop her, man?" the guy asked as he rang up the man's soda.

"I don't know."

"Hey," I said, interrupting. I smiled as they both looked at me. "I know this is a long shot, but could that *Jessica* you two are talking about be Jessica Sanders?"

The guy with the soda took a sip through his straw and furrowed his eyebrows at me. "No. I know the Sanders girl, though. Why?"

"I just need to ask her a question."

"And who are you?" The guy behind the counter asked.

"I'm Micah. I just have a question about an old boyfriend she had."

The guy with the soda looked over my shoulder and saw the growing line. "Let's talk outside. I'll give you what you need." He turned around and paid the cashier.

"Hey," I said, coming out of the gas station.

He turned around. "I don't know where Jess lives, but I will tell you this, though: she works over at the hotel restaurant down by the water. She's been pretty busy there lately, so you're bound to see her if you go there. She's a bartender."

I nodded. "Thank you," I said.

"No problem," he replied.

Going back to my truck, I smiled and looked to heaven as I thanked God for the coincidence. I pumped my gas and took off, heading for the only hotel on the ocean front that also had a restaurant. Hurrying from the parking lot, I headed straight through the hotel lobby and went into the restaurant.

"How many are in your party?" a young girl asked at the hostess station up front.

Shaking my head, I approached her. "I'm not eating. I'm just looking for someone. Jessica Sanders?"

The girl turned and looked into the restaurant. She stood up on her tippy toes as she scanned the room. "She's right . . . there!" Dropping her heels back to the floor, she led me through the crowded restaurant and over to a young brunette woman that looked exhausted and a bit on edge. The hostess said, "This guy was asking for you," and then she went back toward the front of the restaurant.

"Jessica?" I asked, leaning across the bar top.

She lowered an eyebrow. "Yeah? Who are you?" she asked, taking a step back.

"Micah Freeman. I'm here about Blake."

She looked around and came out from the bar. She grabbed my arm and took me through a side door and pushed me outside. Coming out right behind me, she shut the door and asked, "Who are you?"

"I told you! I'm Micah Freeman. What was the meaning of that?"

"You were asking about Blake."

"Yeah," I replied as I glared at her. "I am. I'm friends with his brother, William."

Her eyes appeared to well with tears.

"What?" I asked.

"Nothing. I don't know anything about anything." She turned and grabbed the door handle to go back in.

Pushing on the door, I said, "Please. Just tell me what happened the night he vanished."

She shook her head. "I can't. I have to go."

Jessica went back inside and the door shut behind her. As the door closed, so did my only lead.

Arriving back at my cabin, I found Joe standing in the driveway. I rolled down my window and stuck my head out. "Could you watch out? I'm trying to park."

His eyebrows furrowed as he stepped into the grass to let me park. Getting out of the truck, I scratched my head as I walked up to him.

"How long have you been here waiting for me?" I asked.

"Since I found out."

"Found what out?"

"That you went and talked to the pastor about Charlie, William, Blake and Jessica . . ."

Raising my hands, I said, "I'm just trying to get to the bottom of what is really going on."

Joe pushed me in the chest and I placed a foot behind me to brace myself. "Don't touch me," I said, clenching my jaw.

"I warned you not to go digging. I don't consider myself an aggressive guy, but when you screw with people I care about, you get a different Joe," he said, pushing me again.

My jaw clenched and I said, "Last time I checked, we're in America. I'm free to do what I want."

"Not in this town, you aren't."

He went to push me again, but this time I grabbed his hands and pushed him backward and into the grass, causing him to fall. Looking down at him, I said, "Stop being so protective, Joe. If everybody is innocent, then what's the issue?"

He jumped up to his feet and got in my face. "The issue is you're not looking out for brothers in Christ. You understand what kind of damage this could do to Charlie's reputation? He's a big deal in Ocean Shores. It's damaging to people's reputation whether they are guilty or not." He turned and began to walk away. "Something to keep in mind while you play detective."

Infuriated that he would come at me like that, I went inside my cabin and locked the door. What did he mean when he said 'not in this town'? Was he threatening me? I wasn't sure, but I didn't like the hostility. Did Pastor Clarkson call him and rat me out about coming by the church? There was something not right about all this, and it fueled me to keep on digging.

CHAPTER 16

Waking the next day to a knock on my front door, I put on my robe and headed down the hallway while I rubbed the sleep from my eyes. Getting to the door, I opened it to see a blue car take off from the curb.

"What on earth?" I said, glancing around. I was about to shut the door when an envelope caught my eye on the wood railing that wrapped around my front porch. Grabbing it, I went back inside and shut the door.

Opening the envelope as I walked into the kitchen, I was surprised to see just a blank white card at the bottom. Pulling it out, I flipped it over to find a message.

Meet me at the Humdinger in Hoquiam @ 11am

I wonder if I should go? I thought. Looking over at the clock on the stove, I saw it was just barely after seven. I still had plenty of time to get ready and phone the wife to see what she thought about the mysterious envelope and meeting.

After my morning cup of coffee and a shower, I came out into the living room and called Denise. I filled her in on the recent developments and she began to sound worried.

"People are being sketchy about this, Micah. Maybe that's a sign you should back off."

"And what? Just let Charlie beat William? If I can find the brother, maybe I can help them get reconnected."

"Maybe the brother left for a reason? Have you

thought of that? Maybe the rumor that he murdered the parents is true. Then what? You're searching for a murderer?"

Shaking my head, I said, "I don't feel it's like that, Denise. There's something else going on."

"What time did you say you're meeting this person?"

"At eleven."

"All right. Keep yourself safe."

"I will," I replied.

On the drive along highway 109, I looked out into the pine trees that lined the guard rail for miles and thought about my princess, Jasmine. Thinking back to when she was sitting in the seat right beside me not even a year ago, my eyes began to water. She had been gone only three weeks, but it already felt like an eternity since I saw her last. I thought about how it wasn't anyone's fault that she was gone, but it was just her time to go. That concept was still a struggle to accept without a reason why. I didn't know what God was really up to, but I knew if I kept praying and relying on Him, then He'd lead me in all my ways. After dwelling on Jasmine for a bit longer than I should have, I prayed the rest of the drive into Hoquiam. God was my rock, and in those moments of weakness, I needed to be carried.

Arriving at the Humdinger in Hoquiam, I saw the blue car I saw pull away from my house earlier that morning. A man sat down by the bay on a large rock that was a few feet away from the ledge of the pavement.

Coming to the edge of the pavement, I said in a nervous tone, "Hey."

He turned and looked at me for a moment and then looked back into the bay. His eyes seemed to be focused on one of the large ships that were in port.

"You must be the one that left that note for me."

"Sure am," he replied. He stood up and turned around to face me while he stayed with his feet on the rock.

"Why are you out on that rock?"

He shrugged. "I was attempting to come across as less threatening. Figured this rock was a good place to be." He adjusted his black framed glasses and looked at the pavement I was standing on. "You mind if I . . .?"

"Sure," I said, stepping back.

"Thanks," he said and jumped across the gap between the rock and the pavement. "Let's walk," he said as he began walking.

Following beside him for a few minutes, I became impatient and said, "So . . ."

"Straight to business. I like that. Anyway. I heard you were poking around Ocean Shores about the Johnson family?"

I nodded.

"That's not such a good idea." the guy jumped up onto a log and continued walking along the top of it.

"Hey. I'm not into threats. I'll go, if that's what this is," I replied and turned to leave.

"No! That's not what this is about at all," he said, jumping down from the log. Hurrying across the pavement up to me, he grabbed my shoulder and yanked me around to face him. "Look. I want to help you. I know where Blake is."

"Where is he then?" I asked.

Shaking his head, he said, "I can't tell you that. You

know his parents were killed, right?"

"They were killed?" I looked down at the pavement and shook my head. "Everyone said they were in a car accident."

The guy laughed. "Is that what they're calling murder these days?"

My eyebrows furrowed. "Why would anyone want to kill them?"

The guy turned and began walking again. I joined his side. Stepping onto the sidewalk that led up along the drawbridge that went over the bay, he said, "That's where things get crazy. The Johnsons had found out about what the Pastor, Charlie and a few others were doing at the church."

"What do you mean?"

"I don't have any proof, but from what Blake has told me, the Johnsons knew they were using the church to launder money."

"That's ridiculous. I've known Pastor Clarkson for a while. He doesn't come across like that kind of guy."

"Yeah?" he said, stopping. "What about Charlie? He's a deacon. You already *know* about how wonderful of a guy he is."

"That's true," I replied. Walking over to the railing on the bridge, I laid my arms on the railing and brought my hands together. I shook my head. The mystery guy soon joined my side.

"I know it's hard to process," he said in an understanding and softened tone.

"How could people use a church to do something like money laundering?" I asked, continuing to shake my head.

"It's jacked, right?" he replied. "I have a plan though."

"Okay, but can I meet with Blake first? I need to get him and his brother back together. They're family. The judge would easily give custody to Blake."

The guy shook his head. "They have the judge in their pocket, dude."

"Man, that sucks."

"That's what happens when crooked people get into places of power. Judge Riddick would never allow Charlie's rights to be taken away."

"Why's Charlie even want the kid? You know, if it's all about the money laundering."

He smiled. "The pit goes deeper. When little

William turns eighteen, he's getting two million from an old logging company the parents owned. Get this, there was a condition in the will that he has to live until then or the money would be donated away."

"Why wouldn't Blake just get the money?"

"Blake left town when they died. He didn't come back for fear of what they would do to him."

"How'd the parents know to add the clause about donating the money?"

He shrugged. "I don't know. I do know that Mr. Johnson was a paranoid type of guy. He thought of everything. I mean, why else would he have a clause added to his will stating the kid had to wait until he was eighteen to get the money and be alive?"

"Yeah. You gotta be pretty paranoid. By the way, who are you?" I asked.

"Name's Rick. I'm a friend of Blake. His fear that drove him to leave William and skip town was rooted in his suspicions about what was going on with the pastor and his parents. One evening, he sat at the top of the stairs, hidden from view, as the Johnsons pleaded with the pastor to repent about something. That was weeks before the so-called *accident* they were involved in."

Looking out to the ships in the bay, I shook my head.

"I have a plan though, Micah."

I laughed. "Yeah. You said that. What is this *plan*?"

"It involves you."

Shaking my head, I pulled away from the railing and said, "I don't want to deal with this kind of thing. They killed people!"

Cars went whizzing by behind Rick before he said anything. Then, he spoke. "You're a man of God, just like me. This isn't right—what they did to Blake and William's parents and what they're doing within the walls of the church."

"It's not my job to right the wrongs in the world."

"That doesn't mean you stand idle while sin, corruption and evil unfold before you."

"I'm just a lowly firefighter from Spokane who lost his daughter. I'm not capable of much."

He laughed and threw his hands up. "You're right, Micah. God doesn't use the broken, the battered, the down and out." Rick turned and put his hands in his pockets as he walked past me and headed down the sidewalk, back the way we came.

"Wait," I said. Running up behind him, I said again, this time firmly, "Wait!"

He turned around to me with a grin. "You ready to listen?"

Laughing, I replied, "Yeah. So what's this plan of yours?"

Arriving back to town later that evening, I stopped at the church to see Pastor Clarkson. Parking, I sat in my truck for a moment with trembling hands. Praying, I asked God to quiet my spirit and bring calmness over me in the moment.

Exiting the truck and heading up to the doors of the church, I knocked. I looked back at my truck as I waited for him to answer.

The door wiggled as the pastor began to unlock it, startling me. I smiled at him to mask my nerves. Pushing the door open, he said, "Hey there, buddy, I was just about to call you."

I'm sure you were, I thought to myself as I stepped into the church. "You have any updates for me?" I watched his face to see if I could spot his deception.

"Yeah. I got a lead on Blake."

"Really?" I asked, surprised.

"Yeah. Guess he's out in New Hampshire. Got an address and everything for you." He handed me a piece of paper as we walked into his office.

"How'd you get this?" I asked, looking at him.

"Just made a call," he replied. "Maybe Blake and his brother can finally get reunited. It'd warm my heart to see those two reunite. Just head to New Hampshire and get Blake."

Nodding, I replied, "Me too. Hey, since I'm here, I was wondering if you had any extra tracks to hand out? I love carrying a few on me at all times, and I gave my last one away."

He paused as he looked at me for a moment and then said, "Yeah. Let me go grab a few for ya." Standing up, he came around his desk and exited the room.

I looked back quickly to make sure he wasn't there and then got up and went over to his bookcase. I set the small, self-standing cross up on a shelf and pointed it toward the desk.

As I released the cross, Pastor Clarkson came back into the room. "Good one."

"What?" I said, jumping slightly. My heart began racing as he walked across the room.

He laughed. "Scare ya?" he asked, walking over to the shelf in front of me. He pointed to a book on the shelf. "Life with Purpose."

Smiling, my nerves settled and I said, "Excellent book."

"Here are the tracks," he said, handing me the stack of pamphlets.

I took them from him and said, "Thank you, Pastor."

"It's my pleasure to help spread the name of Jesus!" he said as he went and sat down at his desk.

This guy is some sort of twisted, I thought to myself as I put the tracks in my back pocket. Rubbing my hands together, I raised my eyebrows and said, "Guess we're done here."

He nodded and I turned to leave. "Hey, Micah?" he said, freezing me in my tracks.

"Yeah?" I asked, turning back around to him.

"You okay?"

"Yeah," I replied with a smile.

"Good." His concern seemed genuine and it confused me.

Hurrying out of the church, I called Rick on my way to my truck in the parking lot. I could hardly keep my hands from shaking from being so nervous. I waited for him to pick up the other end.

"Get it done?" he said.

"Yep. Right on the bookshelf."

He let out a relieved sigh and said, "Good. Now we wait."

"How long?"

"As long as it takes for them to incriminate themselves. I'll be in touch."

Click.

CHAPTER 17

Walking the shoreline the next day after my

morning Bible study and prayer, I admired the

sunrise as it rose over the horizon. Even though I

had come out to walk the beach several times since I

arrived in town, it still reminded me of God and all

His wondrous glory.

Laughter came from further inland, and I looked

over to see that it was William. My smile grew as he

stood waving at me.

"Hey," I said suspiciously as I looked past him.

As I walked over to him, he said, "Don't worry about Charlie. He has a meeting at the church this morning."

"Oh," I replied as I pulled out my cellphone. I began texting Rick to let him know a meeting was in progress. "Charlie been okay toward you lately?"

William looked out to the ocean and ignored my question entirely, responding with, "You're right. The sunrise is beautiful, Mister."

Looking over at the horizon, I nodded. Putting a hand on William's shoulder, I said, "God gives us sunrises and sunsets to remind us there is always tomorrow, and each day is new." Bending a knee, I looked at William and said, "Everything is going to be okay. I promise."

He forced a smile that lasted for a second and then said, "I know. God's Word promises me that." He turned back to the sunrise and continued to smile.

Seeing Denise's name flash across my cellphone

around one o'clock that afternoon caused me to suspect something was amiss.

"What's going on?" I asked hearing her crying on the other end.

She sniffled and then said, "I sent you a picture just a few minutes ago."

"Let me call you back. I can't get pictures while on the phone."

"Okay."

Hanging up, I pulled up the picture she sent.

My phone buzzed and the image loaded on the screen.

It was an acceptance letter for Jasmine into Eastern University, the college we wanted to her to attend.

My eyes filled with tears as that dreadful clamping of my throat came back to me instantly. Crying, I dropped my phone on the couch and went into the kitchen.

I began splashing cold water into my face from the faucet.

She had applied.

She wasn't going to leave.

Why didn't she say anything?

My chest tightened as I turned the faucet off. After toweling my face off and collecting myself, I went back into the living room and called Denise.

"You didn't know?" I asked.

"No," Denise squeezed out. She sobbed for a moment and then composed herself. "She didn't hate us, Micah."

I smiled and said, "No, she didn't."

While reading through my Bible a bit later, my phone rang. Setting the Bible down on the coffee table, I picked it up to see that it was Rick.

"What'd you find out?"

He let out an exasperated sigh and then finally said, "Nothing. They figured it out."

"The camera?"

"Yeah. They took the battery out."

"Okay. What's the plan now?"

"We have to come up with one. I didn't have a backup plan."

"No. No more plans, just get me to Blake. I need to

talk to him. They're going to talk to—"

A knock on my door interrupted me.

"Who's that?" Rick asked.

"I don't know. I'll call you back."

Getting up off the couch, I headed to the front door and answered it. It was Pastor Clarkson.

"Hi, Pastor," I said, keeping a hand on the door.

He shook his head and jarred the door open, pushing it. Stepping inside, he continued into the kitchen. "Don't try to play me, Micah. I know it was you who planted it." He set down the cross on the countertop as he turned around to face me. His face looked weighted with guilt as he let out a sigh and went over to the living room. As he sat down on the couch, he said, "It all started innocently."

Coming into the living room, I sat on the edge of the recliner and listened.

He shook his head and said, "It started a few years back when attendance started to dwindle." He paused, sounding hesitant to continue. "Charlie knew this guy that used to be in the mafia in Brooklyn. The whole money laundering thing was supposed to get us a cut and just help the church get by while we—"

"Did you ever mention the financial struggle to the congregation?"

"Oh, yes. Heavens, yes. Several times, in fact." He shook his head and raised his eyes to meet mine. They watered as he continued. "Nobody cared. Or at least, nobody could afford to care the way we needed."

"God did, and the way you handled it wasn't right."

"It wasn't right." He sniffed. "Things got really bad when the pressure grew from the group we were cleaning the money for."

"What group?"

He shrugged. "I don't know who they are. Just know they were putting pressure on Charlie to increase the amounts we were donating weekly to the fake charity."

"You guys couldn't stop?"

"Charlie didn't want to. He liked the increased amounts because it meant a better profit on the back end."

"For the church?"

The pastor looked down and brought his hands

together as more tears started to come. Shaking his head, he said, "No. We were all taking a cut."

"You and Charlie?"

"Yeah. And a couple of the other deacons."

"Jeez," I replied, leaning back into my chair. "This is bad. Really bad."

"I know," he replied, looking up at me.

"Why are you telling me all this?" I asked.

"I wanted to confess. I don't want to hide anymore."

"Why now?"

"Seeing that camera yesterday . . ."

"Yesterday?"

"Yeah. I knew it wasn't mine when you were standing at my bookshelf. I've had the same stuff up on that shelf for years. How do you think Charlie recognized it so easily today?"

"Why leave it for Charlie?"

He shrugged. "I needed to let the whole thing fall apart. Hoped he'd have a change a heart."

"Ahh." *Rick's plan was stupid*, I thought to myself.

"Anyway. When I saw it, I knew you were already onto me. Really, I felt relieved. You gave me a reason to do this. Confess it all and turn myself in."

"What about the judge? Won't he just release you?"

"What? Why would he do that?"

"My contact says you guys have the judge in your pocket."

"That's not true. Charlie and he are good friends, but it's not that kind of thing. We're men of God, not hardened criminals."

"That makes sense," I said.

"Sorry. I shouldn't call myself a man of God anymore."

My heart softened—divinely inspired, I'm sure of it. Looking at the broken pastor, I said, "God forgives us. What y'all did wasn't good. But that doesn't mean God can't forgive it."

Shaking his head, he looked at me. "I don't know about that."

"I do."

I could suddenly hear police sirens in the distance. They grew louder and louder. I looked at the Pastor. "You called?"

"Yeah. Right before I knocked on your door."

Standing up, he extended a hand out to me. I shook his hand and his lips trembled as he became more nervous. We could hear the cops getting out of their cars outside and approaching the door.

A knock came on the door. Muffled, I could hear the cop on the other side. "Mr. Freeman. We're here for the arrest of a Dennis A. Clarkson."

"That's my cue," the pastor said. Turning, he went to the door and opened it. "That's me," he said, turning around to face me as he put his hands behind his back for the cops to cuff him.

Watching as the cops hauled him out to the police cruiser, I couldn't help but admire the man in a way. That took guts and strength to give himself up like that. Rick's amateur plan didn't even work; he could have easily gotten away.

Going back inside, I sat down and called Rick, letting him know the news about the Pastor.

"That's a little strange. He just folded, confessed and turned himself in?"

"I know, right?"

"Hmm. Did he mention anything about Charlie turning himself in?"

"No," I replied.

"Let's hang tight and see what Charlie does."

"What about the judge not being in his pocket?
Can't Blake just get his brother now?"

"I don't know what Blake would want to do."

"All right."

"We'll see what happens. Just relax. It's not over yet."

After getting off the phone with Rick, I phoned
Denise. She was relieved to hear that the pastor had
turned himself in, but she was worried.

"And Charlie? What about him, Micah?"

"I don't know . . ."

"You didn't think about that and what would
happen with William."

"No, I didn't." Getting up, I grabbed my keys from
off the counter and headed for the door. "I'm going
down to their house."

I hung up with Denise and hurried down the street
in my truck. My heart pounded as I headed down
toward William's house. Thoughts of Charlie hurting
William again raced through my mind. I prayed God
would protect him.

Arriving to the house, I made haste to the front door
and knocked. There was no answer. I knocked again.
Again there was no answer.

"Where are you?" I said out loud as I turned around and thought of William.

Walking back out to my truck, a black Town Car pulled up next to my truck and stopped. A window went down, and the man I had seen from the church the other day stuck his head out the window. "You made a serious mistake." He moved out of the way of the window to roll it up, and I saw a glimpse of William. He was bound and gagged, struggling to move as the window rolled back up. I ran out to the car, but it took off down the street before I could catch the plate numbers.

"Please protect him, Lord!" I pleaded as I looked up to the sky. "Please . . ." Stopping in the middle of the street, I called the police and let them know what I had seen. They said they'd be on the lookout for the car.

CHAPTER 18

Getting back over to my place, I saw Joe sitting on

my front porch. *Not this again*, I thought to myself

as I got out of my truck. I slammed my truck door

shut and said, "Go home, Joe. I don't want to hear

it."

He shook his head. "You were right about the

pastor." Standing up, he continued, "I owe you an

apology."

"Ah. You must have heard," I replied as I walked

over to the porch.

"Yep, I was a bit skeptical until I saw Charlie blazing down Ocean Shores Boulevard looking freaked out. Take it he's in on this too?"

"How long ago did you see him?"

"I don't know, like five minutes ago. Why?"

Turning, I ran back to my truck.

"Micah," Joe shouted from the steps.

Stopping as I opened the door, I looked back at Joe.

"Can I go with you?"

"No, I'm okay."

He hurried over to the truck and said, "These people mean a lot more to me than to you. Please let me go. I might be able to help."

"All right. You can come. Just don't question my decisions or what I'm doing."

He nodded and climbed in the passenger side.

We hurried down Ocean Shores Boulevard and then out to Highway 115 that led out of town. The truck was relatively quiet as we drove for the first ten minutes. Then, he broke the silence. "Hard to believe," he said.

"Yeah. It's all kind of weird for a church."

He shook his head. "These guys have been leaders for a long time."

I looked over at him for a moment and then back at the road. "Don't let it get you down. People make mistakes, man."

"Not like this. Not Christians, anyways."

"C'mon. Christians aren't perfect."

"No. But they aren't corrupt."

"Corruption happens. We can't let the troubles of this world take our joy of God away." The words sank into my soul as they rolled off my tongue. I glanced over at Joe again; he nodded as he seemed to be deep in thought. "Bad things happen. Even to Christians."

"You're right. Just hard to chew." He appeared to think for a moment longer, and then he suddenly smacked the dash. His eyes watered and he looked over at me. "Was my dad in on this?"

"I don't know, man," I replied, shaking my head as we rounded the bend in the highway. "Not sure how many deacons or people are part of this."

"Hey! There's Charlie!" Joe said, pointing out the windshield at the gray sedan in front of us.

Getting to the left side of the lane we were in on the two-lane highway, I checked for oncoming traffic. There wasn't any, so I pulled over into the left lane and pulled up beside Charlie's car.

Joe rolled down his window and started yelling at him. "Pull over!"

Charlie yanked on his steering wheel and smashed into the truck, sending me veering off the road. We hit the gravel and nearly hit the guard rail, but I was able to pull back onto the road without losing much speed. A semi-truck was coming down the road then, so I got back behind Charlie.

"He's not stopping," Joe shouted over at me.

"We'll follow him," I said confidently. My phone rang. Pulling it out, I tossed it over to Joe. "Who is it?"

Looking at the screen, he replied, "Rick?"

I reached over and grabbed the phone and answered. "I'm following Charlie."

"Don't let him out of your sight."

"I won't."

"Did he have William?"

"I don't know, but he could be leading us to the

dude that does."

"What dude?"

"I don't know! A dude! Pudgy. Short hair. Balding. I saw him at Charlie's house when I went over there looking for him."

"Riccardo," Rick said confidently.

"Who's Rick?" Joe asked from beside me, interrupting the phone call.

"He's helping," I replied, pulling my face away from the phone for a moment.

"Ask him if my dad was involved in all this."

"What's his dad's name?" Rick asked, hearing the question.

"Ralph Edmunds," I said.

"Doesn't ring a bell. Hey. Keep your eyes on Charlie; I'm going to work on finding Riccardo."

"The police are already on the pursuit."

Rick laughed. "Okay. I'm still going to be looking for him. No offense to the men in blue, but . . ."

Charlie suddenly veered off the road and down a gravel road to the right. He did it so quickly that I didn't have time to react and follow. Looking into my rearview mirror for a moment, I saw it was clear and slammed on my breaks. "I gotta go," I said to Rick and hung up the phone. Tossing it onto the dash, I put my arm over the bench of the truck seat and threw the truck into reverse. Backing all the way up to the turn Charlie took, I put the truck into drive and began down the gravel road.

The cab of the truck rattled as we went down the bumpy road and Joe clutched onto the door. "I don't like this . . . I have a bad feeling."

"It's fine." I leaned down to the seat and pulled the nine millimeter that I had strapped under the driver's seat. Handing it to him, I said, "God and guns are the only protection we need."

He set it down on the seat between us and said, "You go ahead and handle the gun; I'll do the praying."

Driving down the path, we came into a thick patch of trees and the gravel turned to dirt. A few minutes later, we emerged out of the trees and arrived at a log cabin by the North Bay shoreline. Smoke billowed from the chimney and Charlie's car sat parked out front.

Joe looked over at me. "I'm going to hang back and keep praying. You know. Safely in the truck."

"You offered help. You're going to help." I smiled. Parking the truck, I grabbed the gun and put it in my belt behind my back and got out.

Joe got out a moment later. He came around to the front of the truck and to my side. Leaning into my ear, he said, "Something's off here. It's gotta be a trap. Right?"

"I'd suspect," I replied in a quieted voice. Taking a step toward the log cabin, I moved my hand to my back and relaxed my palm against the gun. Praying, I asked God for confidence and wisdom. My heart pounded as I approached the front door of the cabin.

"I'll be back here," Joe said, staying at the truck.

I nodded back at him and continued. Arriving at the front of the cabin, I knocked on the screen door. The metal rattled, and then slowly the door creaked open, but nobody was there.

Peeking in, I could see a gold haze of dust shine through the kitchen window. "Charlie?" I called out, keeping one hand behind my back on the gun. "Just want to chat."

No response.

Turning around, I looked at Joe.

He shrugged. Then his eyes went wide just as a shot went off behind me.

I jumped off the steps and staggered backward away from the cabin. It was Charlie. He'd shot a bullet through the mesh in the screen door. Keeping the door shut, he said, "You'd better leave before the not-so-nice people show up. They won't give you a warning shot."

"We just want to chat," I said, heart still pounding.

"You don't understand," Charlie replied, shaking his head as he dipped his chin. "You need to leave."

Suddenly, the Town Car I had seen at Charlie's appeared through the woods and came up to park beside Charlie's vehicle.

"Well, well . . ." Riccardo said, getting out of the car. Looking over at him, I saw William wasn't in the back anymore, just a big, bald Hawaiian driver. "I just want the kid," I said.

Riccardo shook his head as he walked toward me. His driver got out and stood with his arms crossed, remaining near the car.

"You made this easy for me," he said, walking up to

me.

He pulled a revolver from his coat and pointed it at my chest.

"Don't," Charlie said, pushing the screen door open and coming outside.

He looked over at Charlie with furrowed eyebrows. "You folding too? Like that pathetic pastor of yours?"

"There's just no reason to kill him."

"You churchies are all the same," Riccardo replied. He raised his gun to Charlie and pulled the trigger. He fell to the ground and began squirming as he grabbed his stomach where he had been shot. My heart raced as I moved my hand behind my back to grab my gun, waiting for the perfect moment to draw it.

Riccardo walked up to Charlie on the ground and pointed the gun at his head.

Suddenly, a ringing in my ear interrupted my train of thought and then a pulsing sensation came from the side of my arm. Looking down, I saw that I had been grazed with a bullet. Lifting my eyes, I saw the smoking gun of Riccardo's driver, the Hawaiian.

Then I fell to the ground.

"Micah!" Joe shouted.

Looking over to the truck as I lay on the ground, I saw Joe dart over to the driver that shot me. I watched him wrestle the giant to the ground.

Riccardo watched but didn't interrupt.

Then the driver's gun went off.

I didn't know or couldn't tell who was shot. Then, Joe stood up.

Riccardo became enraged and turned to Charlie. Putting a bullet in his head, he killed him.

Then, Riccardo walked over to me and pushed the revolver into the side of my head. His eyes were full of evil and his face was red hot as he placed his finger on the trigger.

I prayed for my wife and William, that God would watch over them.

Then he pulled the trigger.

The gun jammed.

Looking over, I saw Joe as he pulled the trigger of the gun he had taken from the driver. The shot hit Riccardo in the chest and he crashed to the ground. Joe sprinted over and leaped through the air,

landing on top of Riccardo. He began to punch him
repeatedly in the face.

"Joe! Stop!" I shouted from the ground as I tried to
sit up.

He paused and looked over at me.

"This isn't you. Stop."

"This scumbag doesn't deserve to live!" he lashed out
at me.

"Give him grace, not what he deserves. You already
shot him."

Letting go of Riccardo, Joe rose to his feet. Coming
over to me, he bent a knee, and with trembling
hands that were bloodied, he inspected my wound.

"You're lying here bleeding and still preachin'?" He
laughed.

I smiled at him. "God still died for him."

"True. We need to get you to a hospital."

"Hold on," I grunted. I began to inch toward
Riccardo, but Joe helped me to my feet and the rest
of the way. "The bullet only grazed me."

"No. It's in your arm."

"Oh." Dropping to my knees at Riccardo's side, I
pushed the thoughts of the wound out of my mind

and asked Riccardo, "Where's the boy?"

He tightened his lips together firmly and then spat blood into my face. He glared at me as blood trickled down the side of his face.

"Do one good thing in your life!" Joe shouted over my shoulder.

I put my hand up to Joe. "Stop." Turning back to Riccardo, I wiped the blood he spat at me off and said, "That little boy is innocent in all of this."

He let out a cough and covered his mouth as he turned over on his side. Pulling his hand away, he began to tremble as he saw dark blood smeared across his palm. His face softened as he looked me in the eyes. "I don't want to die."

Putting my hand on his shoulder, I said, "Death has lost its sting when you are saved. Have you made a commitment to Christ, Riccardo?"

He shook his head and let out a laugh under his breath. "God would never let a soul like mine into heaven. I've done terrible, terrible things. I'm not a good person."

"Being a good person doesn't get you into heaven."

"He's right, Micah. He doesn't have a chance at

heaven!" Joe shouted. Standing up and ignoring the pain that crept on the outside of my mind, I got in Joe's face.

"You'd better shut your mouth, man! This guy is dying, and we're obligated to share the truth! Grace!" Joe's hardened face softened as he nodded. Turning back to Riccardo, I got back down on my knees and looked him in the eyes. I could see the fear he felt in his soul.

"God doesn't want a guy like me," Riccardo said.

"That's not true," I said. "God's a good father and He loves you, regardless of what you've done. If you only accept Jesus as your Lord and Savior, you will be able to go to heaven."

Riccardo began crying and his lips trembled as he directed his eyes to the sky. "Lord!" he cried out. "Save me . . . I don't deserve You. But please, please . . . save me!"

"Ask His forgiveness," I added gently.

He sniffed and continued, "Please forgive me of the—" Tears came pouring out of his eyes more and more as he choked up on the words he was trying to speak. "Please forgive me of the wickedness I have done." He coughed again. More dark blood came up. My eyes watered as I pulled Riccardo close to me. Putting my face into Riccardo's shoulder, I held him close and said, "You're going home to paradise today, Brother."

As I let go of Riccardo, he drew his final breath and said, "He's being taken to Billings . . ." Then Riccardo was gone from earth.

Joe came and helped me up to my feet. "I can't believe you did that," Joe said leading me over to the truck. "I could have never—"

"Hey." I looked up at him and said, "You did. You stopped when I said to give him grace."

He nodded as we got to the truck. Opening the passenger side door, he helped me in. Checking my arm, I saw the blood gushing and the pain I had so easily ignored was inching itself back into my mind. "Grab the shirt on the floor," I said with a shake of my head.

He grabbed the blue shirt and made a tourniquet for my arm. Hearing sirens approaching in the distance, I breathed a sigh of relief.

Rick showed up in his car and rushed over to me.

Looking at me for only a second, he shouted back at the EMT and said, "Get over here!"

"How are you here?"

"I followed the sirens."

I nodded and said, "William is heading to Billings."

"How'd you figure that out?"

"Riccardo told me."

"Okay. I'm going to head back to the police station and wait there for William to get picked up."

The EMT pushed by Rick and began inspecting my arm. Rick pulled away and ran back to a cruiser. Another EMT came over and looked at Joe. Looking up to the sky, I thanked God that I was there; even if it was a horrific scene, a soul was saved that day.

CHAPTER 19

Getting out of surgery late that evening, I opened my eyes to find Joe asleep in the chair beside my bed. Smiling, I stayed put and relaxed while I praised God for his mercies that day. God had protected my life from being taken, and I was thankful beyond measure for that and for Blake and William soon being able to reunite.

Taking the disposable water cup that sat next to my hospital bed, I drank the contents and then crinkled it up and tossed it over at Joe. It smacked him in the face, waking him up.

He blinked his eyes open, and when he saw I was awake he leaped up from his chair. "Micah!" he said, smiling. "How are ya feeling?"

"I'm okay," I replied. "Did they find William yet?"

"They got him. He's on his way back to Ocean Shores from the Tri-Cities."

I let out a relieved sigh and smiled a grin from ear to ear. What a blessing he was alive and well.

"You seem awfully chipper," Joe admitted at my bedside.

"God is good."

"Dude. You could have died today!" Joe said with a bit of agitation. "We saw people dropping around us like flies. Toss in the fact that you just lost Jasmine—"

"What's your point?" I asked, interrupting him.

He put his hands up and dropped them to his side and said, "I don't get how you can quickly turn so positive."

I laughed. "God's amazing. He's been carrying me through it all, man. His power is shown to me over and over again. I'll admit it: when I lost Jasmine I was shaken to my core, but He found me. He carried me. I was a sheep that strayed from the flock and He came and rescued me."

"You don't need to preach to me." He walked around the end of my bed and over to the hospital window. "I'm a Christian . . . I killed someone today. Not just one, but two people."

"You also helped lead one to Christ."

He turned and looked at me. "That horrible man?" He laughed and looked back out through the window. "He isn't going to heaven."

"Knock it off, Joe."

"What?" He came over to my side and continued, "You can't just be a horrible person and get into heaven."

"If you repent and accept the Lord into your heart, you better believe you can. Don't forget the *talents* story," I replied.

"Why would God let horrible people into heaven?" Joe asked. "I guess I'm just confused."

"He sees Jesus when He looks at us that are saved. It doesn't matter how bad your sin is. There is no difference between telling a lie once or killing someone. Sin is sin is sin. If you repent and accept the Lord as your Savior, you're in."

"I don't believe that," he said sharply.

"C'mon. Grace is what God gives; Justice is what we deserve. Nobody is perfect, and if you make one mistake in this life, you are guilty and deserving of Hell. Nobody is perfect, and we all need Jesus."

Joe nodded. "Just hard to let myself be grouped in with a cold-blooded killer."

"Don't view it like that then. View it like he's a human who has made mistakes. If you tell one lie, you are a liar. If you look at someone lustfully that isn't your spouse, you're an adulterer. It's a matter of the heart, not outwardly acts."

"All right. All right. I get that. Maybe I'm just freaked out about killing people?"

"Yeah. That makes sense. I can't argue with you on that."

He laughed. "Before today, I've maybe shot a gun once in my life. Today, I killed two people and saw a third get killed. Not just a person, but one of the men of God I looked up to for decades. Then, I watched a good friend get shot. Oh, toss in the fact that I found out the men I spent over the last decade looking up to were crooks."

"I bet you're pretty rattled."

"Yeah, man. I'm pretty shaken up!" Joe put his hands on the railing of my bed and clutched as he leaned his head over and dipped his chin to his chest. He looked up at me and said, "It's hard to not just feel so mentally screwed up right now."

"Have you talked to Betty?" I asked.

"No," he replied, letting go of the bed. He began pacing and said, "Tell her I shot two people and—"

"Go home and talk to her," I said. "Sit her down and just lay it all out. It's not a phone call type of thing."

"Okay. I told your wife over the phone . . . she needed to know you were going into surgery. Sorry."

"Oh, jeez," I said, shaking my head.

"She's on her way over," he said as I pulled the hospital room's phone over toward me. He walked over and helped me get it closer to me.

"Denise has to be freaking out," I said as I began to dial.

"Sorry."

"It's okay." The phone began ringing and I looked at Joe. "Go home and see your wife and family."

He nodded and headed for the door. As he was in the doorway, I called out to him.

"Joe," I said. He turned and looked at me. "Pray that God gives you peace. It's going to be hard, but it's Him who can give you peace of mind."

He nodded. "Thanks."

Denise came on the line in a panic. "How is he? Is he okay? I'm driving as fast as I can."

"Honey. Calm down a little bit. I'm fine and resting."

"Oh, thank goodness."

"Please slow down. Don't get yourself killed by driving so fast."

She began crying. "I was so worried about you."

"Did Joe fill you in on what happened?"

"He only said you were in an accident and went into surgery. Didn't go into detail. My mind has created some pretty insane scenarios."

"I'm sure what actually happened will be far crazier than anything you came up with . . ."

"Tell me."

"I'd rather have waited for you to get here, but I'll go

ahead and tell you now."

CHAPTER 20

Denise arrived at the hospital sometime during the wee hours of the morning. I didn't hear her come in, but I did wake up later that morning to find her asleep in the chair by my bed. I smiled as I looked at her; she looked like an angel. Even though I had seen her only a week earlier, it had felt like it had been years.

An hour went by before my nurse came in to check on my vitals and give me a dose of medicine for the pain. As she talked to me, Denise woke up and I leaned to see past the nurse and lay my eyes on my wife.

She smiled at me.

"Are you listening to me?" the nurse questioned.

"Change the gauze three times a day. Got it."

She turned to Denise and said, "It's important."

"Okay. I'll make sure he gets taken care of," Denise said, looking at the nurse and then over to me. "I'll be with him."

My smile grew and my heart warmed at her words. The nurse left and Denise got up and came over to me. Leaning down, she kissed my forehead and said, "I should have come with you in the beginning."

"It's all right. You seem to be doing a lot better. Plus, I wouldn't have wanted you there yesterday."

She nodded and said, "I've really been turning to God more than ever before, and I used to think I had a close relationship with Him."

"That makes me so happy to hear."

"I never knew how much I didn't rely on God until—"

I raised my hand and touched hers. "I know."

She smiled. "I love you."

"I love you too," I said while rubbing her hand.

"Are you hurting?"

"I'm okay." The phone rang in my room. I reached over and grabbed it. "Hello?" I said, bringing it to my ear.

"Hello, this is Officer Craig from the police department. Are you the guy who called in with the tip for finding William?"

"Yes, that's me, Micah. How is William?"

"William's here at the station. He's pretty shaken up, but he's okay."

"Thank you, Jesus," I said out loud, praising God.

"Jesus? You mean Lieutenant Daniels. He found him. And you, for getting Riccardo to tell you before he kicked the bucket."

Shaking my head, I said, "No. Thank you, Jesus. He's the one who deserves the credit. It was *after* Riccardo gave his life to Christ that he told me where William was."

"Interesting," Officer Craig replied. "Well, we have a few more questions for William to see if he can tell us anything else about his captors, but after that we

will be releasing him to Rick, who's here at the
station with him."

"Sounds good. Can I talk to Rick for a moment?"

"Sure." The police officer put me on hold until Rick
got on the phone a few moments later.

"Hey."

"Blake on his way?" I asked. "Or what's the plan?"

"What about we meet you at William's old place?"

"All right. I'll head there after they release me from
the hospital here shortly."

Hanging up with Rick, I broke the news to Denise
and she was just as happy as I was about William
finally getting his big brother back after being gone
for so long.

As we waited for me to get released, Denise and I
spent the rest of the time playing cards and praising
God. As Denise helped me into the car after I was
released, I sat in the passenger seat and looked at
her with a warm, affectionate smile.

"What is it?" she asked.

"God."

"What about Him?" she asked, holding the door
open as the nurse took the wheelchair back toward

the hospital.

"He knew. Knew I was going to come to Ocean Shores . . . knew I'd take the steps I did."

"Yeah."

"I was so stuck in my grief, I didn't ever realize that He was still working and doing things I knew nothing about. He worked it together for good."

"It's hard to swallow the idea that Jasmine dying was part of His plan."

I shook my head. "I don't think He planned it, I think He knew it would happen and He worked it for His glory. He led me out here and to meet William."

Denise looked up at the sky and said, "He's always working."

"Yes, He is."

She smiled at me, closed the door and came around the front of her car and got in.

Arriving at William's house, we knocked on the front door. There was no answer, so we journeyed to the back of the house. Through the tall grass on the sand dunes, we saw William running up the beach. Taking Denise by the hand, I walked with her down the path that led over the sand dunes and down to the shore. As we walked out to the beach, William looked over and stopped as he saw us. Sprinting over to us, sand kicked up behind him as he approached. Smiling as he arrived, he asked, "Where's Blake?"

"What?" I replied. "I thought he was with you? Rick said he was on his way."

"Rick said he was with you . . ."

"Where's Rick?"

"I'm right here," he said from behind Denise and me. We turned and stood next to William as he walked down the last few steps and into the sand. "Blake's not coming." He turned and looked up at the beach house as he continued, "The answers you need are in there. In the office. Check the desk." Rick put his hands in his pockets and began walking down the beach.

"No," I said. Running across the sand and up to Rick, I grabbed his shoulder. "Stop, Rick. Where's Blake? Why isn't he coming now? We had an understanding!"

He swung his shoulder back, releasing from my hold. "He's dead!"

"I'm calling the police!"

"Why?"

"They released him thinking that you were bringing him to his brother. You lied to the cops!"

Rick shook his head. "You don't know what you're talking about, Micah! I'm the kid's uncle."

"What?"

"Yeah. I'm his uncle. That's why I tried to keep my distance through all of this. Everybody in town knows that. I didn't want to take in a kid after the parents died, and Charlie took him in. I got word from Blake's old girlfriend that you were sniffing around and I took advantage of it. I wanted justice for Blake and his parents, and for that kid to have a good home. You know, a family that loves him. I think you'll do that."

Dumbfounded, I turned and saw William and Denise in the distance. They didn't hear a word. Looking back at Rick as he continued walking away, I said, "Why didn't you want to take him?"

Rick came back over to me and yelled, "I didn't have the time nor the energy for a kid! I didn't want that life! And Charlie only did it for the money."

"What was all that *man of God* talk?" I asked.

He laughed. "Since when did being a man of God make you perfect?" He turned and continued down the beach.

"One last question for you, Rick."

He stopped and turned around.

"How come William didn't recognize you?"

"I never saw him more than a couple of times in his life. I'm free to go now?"

I nodded.

He turned and left.

Walking back to Denise and William back near William's house, I shook my head.

"Where's my brother?" William asked.

I bent down on my knees and met him eye-level. My eyes watering, I said, "Your brother is in heaven."

William almost darted away, but I caught him in my arms and pulled him in close. He began squirming and wiggling as he screamed. Denise dropped to her knees and her eyes began to water.

"I want my brother!" William shouted as he cried. "I want my brother! He was supposed to come for me!"

"I know . . . I'm sorry," I said as he slowed his squirming. "We're going to take care of you."

He sniffed and said, "What happened to him? My brother?"

Looking up at the beach house, I thought of what Rick said about the office. "Let's go find out."

Inside the office in the house, I began to lift papers and move documents that were strewn out across the desk. Then I began to go through the drawers. Arriving at the last drawer, I pulled out a paperweight to find nothing. *Nothing is in this desk! Rick lied!* I thought to myself. Dropping the paperweight back into the drawer, I heard a hollow thump when it hit the wood. Bending at the knees, I knocked on the wood that lined the bottom of the drawer. It sounded hollow. Taking the paperweight, I busted the wood and found a secret compartment underneath. Opening it, I found a stack of papers.

Pulling the bundle of papers out onto the desk, I looked over at Denise and William. I wasn't sure how Rick knew where these papers were, but judging by the looks of them, it was where Charlie kept all his important documents.

I began to thumb through the documents until I arrived to a newspaper clipping. My eyes began to water as I read the words highlighted in yellow.

Blake E. Johnson, 22, of Ocean Shores, died February 2012 as a result of injuries sustained in a motor vehicle accident involving a drunk driver. He was born August 9, 1990 . . .

"What is it, Micah?" William asked.

I pulled my lower lip into my mouth and bit it as I shook my head. "I'm sorry," I said, holding the clipping out for him to grab.

He sighed and took it from my hand. He read what he could of it and then wrapped his arms around me so tight, I felt like he wasn't ever going to let go.

Denise came into the room and up to us as we stood near the desk. As my eyes watered, she put her hand around my back and leaned her head on my shoulder. Bringing her other hand to William, she ran her fingers through his hair and said, "Everything's going to be okay, William."

William brought his arm out from my side and put it around Denise and leaned his head against her as he continued to cry. "Thank you," he said through the tears.

Leaving the house, we all three got in Denise's car and drove back over to the cabin. Joe was sitting on the porch when we arrived. This time I was happy to see him. He didn't look good, though. It looked as though he didn't sleep a wink the night before. Getting out of the car, I walked over to him.

"Hey," he said, looking at me. He flashed a look over at William and Denise and then back to me. "Could we chat?"

"Sure," I said. I walked out to the sidewalk with him.

"You feeling okay?" he asked.

"Yep. What's up?"

"So. There's this thing that I'm trying to figure out. Um. I'm not sure how to go about saying this . . ."

My eyebrows went up as he stumbled over his

choice of words. "I'm not trying to be rude, but I'm in pain. If you could speed this along, it'd be appreciated, buddy."

"I have to ask you something, and I'm scared what you'll respond with."

"Well, if you don't ask it in two point five seconds, I'm go—"

"Will you move to Ocean Shores and run the church?" he asked quickly and then winced as he waited for a response.

I hadn't even entertained the thought. His question did make sense, though, since I had basically destroyed the leadership at Christ Community. "Can I pray about it and get back to you?" I asked.

"Of course," he said, nodding. He seemed relieved. "Thanks for not shooting it down right away."

"I never say *no* right away to a possible opportunity. Especially when it involves God."

"Good," he replied, smiling. Glancing past me, he looked at the two of them and waved, "Nice seeing you again, Denise. And William—glad to see you made it back safely."

They both waved to Joe as I looked back at them. I

smiled and looked back at Joe.

"Betty's going to be home in a minute with some food. I better get back."

"Thanks for coming over."

He nodded and began walking down the sidewalk.

"You can stop by and sit on my porch anytime you want, Joe."

He laughed. "Thanks," he replied. He continued on the sidewalk down to his house.

CHAPTER 21

After explaining the situation to Judge Riddick the next day, he ordered that a temporary guardianship be provided to Denise and me for William. With the custody in place and an official hearing scheduled for a month out, we all three packed up and left for Spokane a week later to attend Kane's wedding. The decision to Pastor Christ Community Church still hung in the air, but a decision hadn't been made on my part. Never being led to be a pastor in my life, I wasn't sure if it was a calling put on my life or not. God hadn't given me clear direction one way or the other.

Pulling up to our house in Spokane, William took his seatbelt off and leaned forward between our seats. "That's your house? It's amazing!"

Denise and I both looked at each other behind William's head. We had a lot of good memories in that house. Sure, there was lots of pain associated with the house, but we were coming into a new period of our grief in which we allowed ourselves to appreciate the time we had. In reply to William, I said, "Sure is, buddy."

Walking inside, I couldn't help but have memories of Jasmine come flooding into my mind. It was different than the last time I was in the house. Instead of a sense of hopelessness, I was filled with a sense of loss, but also gratefulness for the time I did have with her. Watching William climb the stairs as he seemed to be investigating the house, I smiled, admiring his sense of curiosity.

Denise started in on the laundry we had and I began to do the few dishes I found in the kitchen sink.

Hearing the washing machine lid close, I could sense her returning down the hallway. She wrapped her arms around me and rested her head against my shoulders.

"I love being home and your being here again," she said.

"I missed it too," I replied.

"Where's William?" she asked.

"Upstairs investigating." Setting the dishes down, we both headed upstairs to find him and saw Jasmine's bedroom door open.

Denise leaned toward me and said, "I hadn't gone in there since the accident."

"Me neither." I'll admit I was a bit nervous as we walked down the hall. I hadn't set foot in her room since before the accident. It felt like a door I didn't ever want to open again. But we continued down the hall and went in together. I saw William with a dipped chin, standing in the middle of the room.

"What's wrong?" Denise asked as she moved across the carpet over to him.

"This was *her* room, wasn't it?" he asked, looking up at Denise.

Denise didn't respond, but just nodded as her eyes watered.

Coming over to them, I put my hand on each of their shoulders. Looking at William, I said, "Yes. This was Jasmine's room. It'll be your room after we do some cleaning and organizing."

"I had to help Charlie clean my parents' room out after they passed. It was hard. I understand what you're going through."

My eyes went wide. This kid might have been young, but he had some serious life experience under his belt. William turned and looked toward the window in the room. Looking back at me, he raised his eyebrows.

"You can go look."

He smiled and hurried over to the window. Looking outside, he said, "Wow! You can see the neighbor's yard from here!"

I smiled and nodded to him as I put my arm around Denise. She laid her head against my shoulder and put her arm around my back.

"Can we go chop wood?" William asked, turning around from the window. "I see an axe and everything down there!"

I smiled and said, "I can teach you."

"Awesome!" he replied, dashing for the doorway of Jasmine's room. Hearing him hurry down the stairs and head to the back door, Denise lifted her head and looked at me.

"I'm glad you're my husband. You're an amazing man of God and will be great to William."

"Thanks," I replied.

We walked downstairs together and I headed out the back door as Denise split off to the front room. Shutting the door behind me, I found William carrying a log over to the stump. Setting it down, he looked over at me smiling and said, "Show me how it's done."

I laughed and came over to him. Grabbing the axe that was leaning against the stacked wood, I said, "So you hold it like this." Taking the axe into my hands, I set my feet shoulder width apart and showed him how to follow through on the swing of the axe.

We moved the split pieces of wood over to the pile and then put another piece of wood on the chopping block. Standing behind William, I helped him swing the axe and split his first piece of wood.

"Cool!" he shouted as the wood fell to each side of the chopping block. Setting the axe down, he ran over and grabbed the pieces to stack with the others.

After dinner, Denise took William to get him a suit for Kane's wedding the next day. As soon as they pulled out of the driveway to go, I called Cole and asked if he could come over and help me with moving the furniture from Jasmine's room. I knew Denise would be gone for a while and saw it as an opportune time to get it done.

Getting out of his SUV, Cole came up the driveway and into the garage to greet me. Setting the box in my hands down, I embraced him in a hug. He patted my back and shook his head as he released. "How'd the beach treat ya?"

I hadn't told him what had happened yet. "It was interesting."

"God get through to you? You seem different."

I couldn't help but laugh. "Oh, man. You could say God got through to me."

He raised an eyebrow. "What happened?"

We began moving furniture down from Jasmine's room and into the garage. Piece after piece, I told him about all that had happened. As we brought the last piece of furniture—the flowery, purple-colored dresser—down and set it on the garage floor, Cole wiped the sweat from his brow with his arm. He leaned against the top of it and looked over at me. "How do you do it?"

"What?" I asked, wiping the sweat off my face onto the corner of my white tee shirt.

"Always keep the Lord so predominately on your mind. Even though it sounded like you were struggling there for a bit, you got back on track and even witnessed to a dying man."

"My wife plays a vital role. I was in Ocean Shores and wasn't getting back in touch with God like I planned on doing. She helped me refocus. She reminded me of *why* I had gone. It took guts on her part to say something, but I'm better for it."

"So your wife?"

"Yep. She's like my sharpening stone, brother. Behind every great man of God is a woman whom he can rely upon, a woman he can trust, and a woman that loves the Lord with all her heart."

Cole nodded. "Between me and you, I think you should go run that church."

"Really?" I asked.

"Absolutely, Micah. There's no real reason why you can't do it."

"I have no formal education, never went to seminary—"

"C'mon, Moses!" Cole interrupted jokingly.

I broke into a smile and nodded as I laughed. "Good one."

"Seriously, though. Don't let the fear of failing hold you back from experiencing God's will for your life. All this happened for a reason."

"Thanks, man."

CHAPTER 22

Standing next to my comrades from station 9 on a

stage at the Martin Woldson Theater, I looked

across the crowd of people who had come to

celebrate the marriage of Kane and Kristen. My eyes

jumped from face to face in search of my wife and

William. My smile grew when I found them in the

midst of the crowd. I hadn't seen her since I left the

house earlier that morning, so I was missing her. My

wife looked breathtaking in a beautiful yellow dress

with crystal-like gemstones. William looked dashing with his comb over and a dark suit.

William waved up at me and I waved back.

Leaning into my ear, Cole said beside me, "Cute kid."

"Yeah. He's a good boy."

On my other side was Rick. He leaned over and asked, "Who's the kid?"

"Did you miss the conversation we had at breakfast earlier?" Cole asked, looking in front of me at Rick. "Or were you taking another nap, grandpa?"

Rick laughed. "Don't be mad because you're jealous I'm retired. You know that hearing aid I just got a while ago doesn't work too well!"

Cole smiled.

I looked at Rick and said, "He's a kid Denise and I are going to look after now."

His eyebrows shot up. "At your age?"

"Well, yeah."

Shaking his head, Rick said, "Good luck. You'll be over sixty when he graduates high school."

"That's okay. I'll still be younger than you," I replied with a smile.

Kane finally entered the auditorium and hurried down to the stage stairs and up to us.

"Did you have some second thoughts?" Ted asked from beside Rick.

"No," Kane replied with a short and nervous laugh. "Just a few hiccups in the kitchen about the fish and steak. I got it all sorted out."

"All right. Let's do this. We're already ten minutes past three," Cole said.

Kane nodded as he wiped his brow with the sleeve of his tuxedo. "I've never been so shaky in my life." He looked over at Cole and then at me. "Do you think this is a sign or something? Like I shouldn't go forward?" He glanced toward the door of the auditorium.

"No, man. It's not a sign," I said with a hint of laughter, remembering those jitters all too well. Cole put his arm around Kane and said, "It's okay to be nervous. It's a big deal."

Kane looked to the back as the doors opened and his bride appeared. His smile grew bigger than I had ever seen as she began walking down the aisle.

Taking Denise's hand in mine, I led her out to the dance floor in the reception hall. Pulling her in close, we began to sway to the rhythm of the music. As she rested her head against my chest, she let out a giggle.

Looking to see what she was laughing about, I spotted William taking the hand of one of the little girls that were attending.

"He's a sweet boy," Denise said.

"He really is."

"You give any more thought to taking Joe up on the offer?"

"Talked to Cole about it some yesterday."

"And?"

"He thinks it's a good idea."

"He's okay with losing you at the station?"

"Outside the fact I'm set to retire next year, I think he cares more about what God wants than what's good for the station."

"I guess that makes sense." Denise lifted her head and looked me in the eyes. The soft white lights coming from the spinning disco ball reflected in her eyes as she said, "You should do it."

"But what about our house and the pension and—"

"When has God let us down? Ever not provided?" She looked over at William as he slow danced with that girl. "I think it'd be good for him, too. He knows a lot of kids in the church and the people there."

Denise was right. God wasn't one to let us down or not provide. Everything that had happened since Jasmine had passed did so for a reason. Taking the trip to Ocean Shores and waking up early that morning and meeting William—God was working things together all along. "It's going to take a lot of work to rebuild that church."

"I know. I've already acknowledged that."

"Even for you. Being the pastor's wife."

She nodded. "I'll stand by your side no matter what you choose to do, Micah."

I smiled. "How'd I get so lucky to get to call you my wife?"

She beamed with a smile in return and said, "I love you."

"I love you too."

Later in the evening, all the guys from the station were sitting at a few tables that were pushed together when I decided to break the news. Standing up, I tapped my water glass with a piece of silverware to get everyone's attention. Silence fell across the group of guys.

"Hey, all." I looked over at Kane and said, "Sorry to steal your special day with an announcement, but I need to let ya'll know I'm moving to Ocean Shores to live and be the pastor of a church there."

Everybody was hushed for a moment before the Chief stood up. Unable to read his mood as the lighting in the reception hall was low, I waited nervously for his response.

He raised his glass and said, "Everyone know how I was out for the past little while?"

"Yeah. You were on vacation like a month. Slacker," Kane said, grinning.

He smiled and looked down the tables at me. "I wasn't on vacation. I was in the hospital having a triple bypass."

The group of guys gasped.

"Really?" Kane asked.

"You didn't tell us?" Cole added.

"Why didn't you say anything, Chief?" Ted questioned.

Paul tipped his chin to me as he continued. "Micah knew, and he came up to the hospital the morning of the surgery." He paused as everyone looked over at me. "He told me something I'll never forget, and I'll cherish it until the day I die. He said, 'Paul, if you only trust that God has your best interest in mind, you'll find the peace you so desperately need.' I relied upon that statement alone through the recovery process of my operation, and I am blessed to have you as a friend as long as I have. You'll make an amazing pastor, and all I have to say is you'd better call! Here's to your future in Ocean Shores with Denise and little William."

"Thank you," I replied, smiling. My eyes began to well with tears.

CHAPTER 23

The following week we put the house on the

market and began preparations to move. One day I

was out in the garage, working on sorting through

more of Jasmine's belongings, when I came across a

picture of her and her last boyfriend–Austin. My

eyes watered looking at my princess's face. It had to

be one of the last photos she had been in. Glancing

over at Austin, my eyes began to water. I hadn't

reached out or communicated with the kid in any

way since the accident. He had to be devastated.

I went inside and found Denise in the kitchen wrapping dishes in newspaper. "Hey, honey."

"Yeah?" she said as she continued wrapping a plate.

Holding the picture in one hand, I tapped it against the palm of my other and asked, "Have you spoken to Austin since the accident?"

She stopped and looked over at me, then at the picture in my hands. "I spoke to his mother at the funeral, but outside of that, No. Not really."

"Did his mom say how he was doing?"

She shook her head. "No. I didn't ask."

"I think I'm going to meet up with him. Do you have his or his mom's number?"

"Yeah. I have his." She set the plate down and went over to her purse in the living room. As she dug through the purse she asked, "What are you planning to do?"

"Just want to sit down with the kid and let him know I don't blame him for what happened. Ya know?"

She nodded. Pulling out a piece of paper, she came over to me in the kitchen and gave it to me. "That's a good idea."

"I think so too."

Heading back out to the garage, I texted him and set up a time to meet for coffee. He was working a new job at a gas station, but he would be off around five, so we planned on six at a coffee shop downtown.

Almost not recognizing the kid when I arrived at the coffee shop, I walked over to his table and sat down. He looked sad and had a sense of hopelessness in his eyes. "Hey, Mr. Freeman," he said, fidgeting with his cup of coffee in between his hands on the table.

"Austin . . . What happened to you?"

He shook his head and set the cup down, looking away. A tear came out of the corner of his eye and he tightened his jaw. Looking back at me, he said, "I'm not doing so hot."

"Why?"

"I could have done something differently. Could have never met her and she'd be alive. Maybe, um . . . I could have told her not to leave your house." He looked down at his cup and picked it back up.

"It's not your fault."

"It's entirely my fault! I was driving that night!" he slammed his cup down and the coffee shop went silent for a moment as they looked at us.

The crowd turned their attention back to their own activities after a moment and I leaned across the table. "It was her time, Austin. You have to understand that it was nobody's fault."

"I saw you at the funeral. You looked mad, sad and destroyed."

I leaned back in my seat and shrugged. "I was mad, but not at you. I was mad with God for taking my little girl."

He scoffed and shook his head. "You're not anymore?"

Shaking my head, I said, "No, It's not God's fault she died. He only allowed it happen because it was her time. She's in heaven now."

"Heaven." He laughed and shook his head as he kept his eyes on the cup. "Yeah. I'm sure she's floating in the clouds and playing a harp. Oh—And you can't forget she's eating grandma Pearl's famous cookies."

"That's not heaven, but that's an entirely different

conversation. Look—what happened was horrible, and I do wish she hadn't died, but we can't stop our life because of it. She wouldn't want any of us to be miserable, Austin."

"I can't be happy in this life. Ever. She was my world, Mr. Freeman!" He wiped his cheeks of tears and said, "She was the breath in my lungs, the air beneath my wings."

"Look, Austin, you're young."

"That doesn't mean our love wasn't real, dude!"

Leaning in, I said, "I didn't say your love with my daughter wasn't real. I'm just saying that you're still young. There's a lot of life ahead of you. If you loved Jasmine as much as you're declaring, you would want to honor her memory."

He nodded.

"You can do that by enjoying your life. She loved the Lord and was a Biblical born-again Christian. Maybe start there and see what heaven is really about."

He sniffed and said, "Maybe I could see her again in heaven."

"Yeah," I replied with a nod. "With salvation through Jesus Christ alone, you can make it to heaven and see her again someday."

"Then we'll be together forever."

I shook my head. "There isn't marriage in heaven or anything like that. But you can see her again. Just start studying, and you'll figure it all out."

He nodded in agreement. "You know, I've just spent every day since the accident wondering how I could have saved her."

My heart burned with regret for not talking to this kid right after the accident. I just was so focused on myself and my own pain that I couldn't even see the others that were hurting. "That's not good."

"I know that now. You know she applied to Eastern?" He choked up on his words as they came out. "She wanted to go to school where her dad went. She was scared to go to New Jersey. She had already applied before I met her, but she didn't tell you guys. It was a pretty big toss-up in her mind between Rowan and Eastern."

"Why didn't she tell us?"

"She didn't want to disappoint you if she didn't get accepted."

My eyes began to water. "She got accepted."

"Wow."

"She was such a sweetheart."

He nodded in agreement. "I loved her."

"I know you did." Getting into an argument about how young love is dumb and blind wasn't the type of conversation I wanted to have with the kid, so I didn't argue with him on the affection he felt toward Jasmine. "Here's my cellphone number," I said, grabbing a napkin from the holder on the table. Pulling the pen from my pocket, I jotted it down and slid it over to him. "Anytime you need to chat, call me. Anytime you need a break, come see me in Ocean Shores."

He took the napkin and put it in his pocket. "You're moving?"

"Yep. Going to be a pastor."

His eyebrows went up. "Wow. Looks like you're just chugging right along."

"It's been a strange journey to arrive at this point. Denise and I have struggled with losing Jasmine, but God has been there for us all along the way. It's through Him that we are able to have peace and hope."

It looked like something clicked in Austin's head. He said, "I want a relationship with God. Just the thought of it brings me comfort in a weird way."

"He's drawing you to Him, Austin."

"But I don't want Church and the Bible. I don't need that stuff. I'm a good person. Plus, I don't want the commitment."

I could tell he wasn't going to make a decision, at least not on that day, but that didn't stop me from continuing to share as much information as I could about the good news. "If you want a relationship with God, you need the commitment, you need the Bible and you need the Church. The Church is a place where believers gather, and the Scriptures are God's love letter to humanity. The commitment is bringing it all together to one. Let me ask you something, Austin. Why would you not want those?"

"Church is full of hypocrites, and the Bible is full of rules."

Shaking my head, I said, "There are some bad churches out there, but you can't just say you won't go because of some bad experiences you had in life. And as for the Bible's rules . . . they're not in place to hurt you, but to allow the freedom and peace of living a life by design. How God designed it. The Bible isn't just a big ancient book, it's the written words of God Himself. If you have any desire to have a relationship with Him, reading the Bible isn't a requirement . . . it's a necessity."

Austin stood up and extended his hand. "You've given me a lot to think about, Mr. Freeman." He looked me in the eyes, and this time I saw hope. "Take care of yourself, Austin."

Coming in the front door, I saw William sitting on the steps that led upstairs. His head was dipped and he seemed to be bothered by something. As I shut the door behind me, I looked at him and asked, "What's wrong?"

He shrugged and looked up at me. "I'm just sad."

"How come?"

"You lost your daughter. It makes me sad."

I sat down next to him on the step he was sitting on. "It was hard, but God got us through it, just like it was hard for you to live with Charlie and to wait all that time for your brother."

"I guess I just wish she were alive. Seeing all her pictures and stuff around makes me think she would have been a pretty cool older sister. I never had a sister."

I smiled and put my arm around him. "She was a pretty neat kid. You would have liked her, but chances are you wouldn't have ever been with us if everything didn't happen the way it did."

"Can you ever be happy when someone you love dies?" he said bluntly.

"I don't think *happiness* is really the goal. I have the joy of God, though, and I'm okay with how God worked everything out in my life and even in my suffering."

"How's pizza for dinner?" Denise asked, coming into the hallway that connected into the living room and kitchen.

I looked over at William and raised my eyebrows, waiting for him to answer.

"Yes! Pizza!" he said, jumping off from the stairs.

That turned around quickly, I thought to myself as I

smiled and stood up.

"We'll order the pizza. Go head upstairs and take that shower," Denise said.

"Okay!" William hurried up the stairs and into the bathroom while Denise and I headed into the kitchen.

"How'd it go with Austin?" she asked, turning around as we entered the kitchen.

Thinking about how sad he was, I shook my head. "He was sad. Really sad. Overall it went good, though."

"How could it if he was sad?"

"We talked about God and heaven. I think it was good for him to talk about it."

She smiled and came closer, touching my chest.

"See? God has equipped you, Micah. Someone like Austin can sit down and feel better after just one conversation. Your being a pastor makes more and more sense."

"I think I did what anyone would do in that conversation."

She shook her head as she looked me in the eyes. With the sweetest voice, she said, "Look over the time you've had at the station with the guys. The people and lives you've touched. You know, I heard last night at the reception what the Chief was saying about you."

"I don't know, Denise. I'm still fairly nervous about it all."

"I know it doesn't come naturally to tout your abilities, but that's good. Let God be your strength as we go forward with rebuilding this church and starting this new chapter in our life."

I nodded. "I will." Wrapping my arms around her, I kissed her cheek and pressed my head against hers as I held her close to me.

CHAPTER 24

Not even two months after leaving Spokane, we closed not only on the sale of our home in Spokane, but also the cabin in Ocean Shores. With seed money to help renovate William's childhood home, we began to settle into our new life in Ocean Shores. It was Sunday morning, and I was getting ready for church in the bathroom when William walked in. Seeing his reflection in the mirror behind me, I smiled and turned around.

"Hey, Dad—I mean, Micah."

Bending down on my knees, I looked at him and said, "You can call me Dad if you want." Denise walked in and we both looked over at her.

"I do want to. I feel like my first mom and dad would be happy I found new ones that love me, and they wouldn't mind me calling you that." He turned and looked up at Denise. "Can I call you Mom?"

"Absolutely," she replied, smiling.

He grinned and said, "God does answer prayers."

"Oh yeah?" I said.

"That morning I met you on the beach, I had been praying for a new mommy and daddy for a while. I asked God to send me someone who would love me like my old mommy and daddy did."

My eyes began to water and I said, "God does answer prayers." Pulling him in close to my chest, I kissed the side of his head and hugged him.

Approaching the pulpit that morning to preach, I looked across the faces I had become acquainted with over the last couple of months. Some names I knew; some names I hadn't learned yet. Whether I was in Spokane in a pew or Ocean Shores at the pulpit, God and His Word never changed. It was the one absolute in life. The hardships I had endured had one consistent thread through them all: God was always there for me, never changing and everlasting.

My experiences and time spent with the guys at fire station 9 in downtown Spokane would never be forgotten. I believe my time served there equipped me to stand at the pulpit and preach the Word of God today. The trials, hardships and storms that life threw at us were prime examples of how fast life can change, how in a single moment everything we know and love can come crashing down around us. The one constant when it comes to our lives is God, and He alone remains firmly planted. While our worlds collapse and we lose all ability to carry on, it's He who carries us through to an end.

Whether we are amongst the flames or our life is up in smoke, it's God who can bring us out of the ashes and heal us after the fire.

The End.

BOOK PREVIEW

Preview of "The Perfect Cast"

Prologue

Each of us has moments of impact in life. Sometimes it's in the form of *love*, and sometimes in the form of *sadness*. It is in these times that our world changes forever. They shape us, they define us, and they transform us from the people we once were into the people we now are.

The summer before my senior year of high school is one that will live with me forever. My parents' relationship was on the rocks, my brother was more annoying than ever, and I was forced to leave the world I loved and cared about in Seattle. A summer of change, a summer of growth, and a summer I'll never forget.

Chapter 1 ~ Jess

Jess leaned her head against the passenger side window as she stared out into the endless fields of wheat and corn. She felt like an alien in a foreign land, as it looked nothing like the comfort of her home back in Seattle.

She was convinced her friends were lucky to not have a mother who insisted on whisking them away to spend the *entirety* of their summer out in the middle of nowhere in Eastern Washington. She would have been fine with a weekend visit, but the entire summer at Grandpa's? That was a bit uncalled for, and downright wrong. Her mother said the trip was so Jess and her brother Henry could spend time with her grandpa Roy, but Jess had no interest in doing any such thing.

On the car ride to Grandpa's farm to be dropped off and abandoned, Jess became increasingly annoyed with her mother. Continually, her mother would glance over at Jess, looking for conversation. Ignoring her mom's attempts to make eye contact with her, Jess kept her eyes locked and staring out the window. Every minute, and every second of the car ride, Jess spent wishing the summer away.

After her mother took the exit off the

freeway that led out to the farm, a loud pop came from the driver side tire and brought the car to a grinding halt. Her mom was flustered, and quickly got out of the car to investigate the damage. Henry, Jess's obnoxious and know-it-all ten-year-old brother, leaned between the seats and glanced out the windshield at their mom.

"Stop being so annoying," Jess said, pushing his face back between the seats. He sat back and then began to reach for the door. Jess looked back at him and asked, "What are you doing?"

"I'm going to help Mom."

"Ha. You can't help her; you don't know how to change a tire."

"Well, I am going to *try*." Henry climbed out of the car and shut it forcefully. Jess didn't want this summer to exist and it hadn't even yet begun. If only she could fast forward, and her senior year of high school could start, she'd be happy. But that wasn't the case; there was no remote control for her life. Instead, the next two and half months were going to consist of being stuck out on a smelly farm with Henry and her grandpa. She couldn't stand more than a few minutes with her brother, and being stuck in a house with no cable and *him*? That was a surefire sign that one of them wasn't making it home alive. Watching her mother stare blankly at the car, unsure of what to do, Jess laughed a little to herself. *If you wouldn't have left Dad, you would have avoided this predicament.* Her dad knew how to fix everything. Whether it was a flat tire, a problematic science project or her fishing pole, her dad was always there for her no matter what. That was up until her mother walked out on him, and screwed everybody's life up. He left out of the country on a three month hiatus. Jess figured he had a broken heart and just needed the time away to process her mom leaving him in the dust.

Henry stood outside the car next to his mother, looking intently at the tire. Accidentally catching eye contact with her mother, Jess rolled her eyes. Henry had been trying to take over as the *man of the house* ever since the split. It was cute at first, even to Jess, but his rule of male superiority became rather old quickly when Henry began telling Jess not to speak to her mother harshly and to pick up her dirty laundry. Taking the opportunity to cut into her mom, Jess rolled down her window. "Why don't you call Grandpa? Oh, that's right... he's probably outside and doesn't have a cell phone... but even if he did, he wouldn't have reception."

"Don't start with me, Jess." Her mother scowled at her. Jess watched as her mother turned away from the car and spotted a rickety, broken down general store just up the road.

Her mom began to walk along the side of the road with Henry. Jess didn't care that she wasn't invited on the family trek along the road. It was far too hot to walk anywhere, plus she preferred the coolness of the air conditioning. She wanted to enjoy the small luxury of air conditioning before getting to her grandpa's, where she knew there was sure to be nothing outside of box fans.

Jess pulled her pair of ear buds out from the front pouch of her backpack and plugged them into her phone. Tapping into her music as she put the ear buds in, she set the playlist to shuffle. Staring back out her window, she noticed a cow feeding on a pile of hay through the pine trees, just over the other side of a barbed wire fence. *I really am in the middle of nowhere.*

Chapter 2 ~ Roy

The blistering hot June sun shone brightly through the upper side of the barn and through the loft's open doorway, illuminating the dust and alfalfa particles that were floating around in the air. Sitting on a hay bale in the upper loft of the barn, Roy watched as his nineteen-year-old farmhand Levi retrieved each bale of hay from the conveyor that sat at the loft's doorway. Each bale of alfalfa weighed roughly ninety pounds; it was a bit heavier than the rest of the grass hay bales that were stored in the barn that year. Roy enjoyed watching his farmhand work. He felt that if he watched him enough, he might be able to rekindle some of the strength that he used to have in his youth.

While Roy was merely watching, that didn't protect him from the loft's warmth, and sweat quickly began to bead on his forehead. Reaching for his handkerchief from his back pocket, he brought it to his forehead and dabbed the sweat. Roy appreciated the help of Levi for the past year. Whether it was feeding and watering the cattle, fixing fences out in the fields, or shooting the coyotes that would come down from the hill and attack the cows, Levi was always there and always helping. He was the son of Floyd Nortaggen, the man who ran the dairy farm just a few miles up the road. If it wasn't for Levi, Roy suspected he would have been forced to give up his farm and move into a retirement home. Roy knew retirement homes were places where people went to die, and he just wasn't ready to die. And he didn't want to die in a building full of people that he didn't know; he wanted to die out on his farm, where he always felt he belonged.

"Before too long, I'll need you to get up on the roof and get those shingles replaced. I'm afraid one good storm coming through this summer could ruin the hay."

Levi glanced up at the roof as he sat on the final bale of hay he had stacked. Wiping away the sweat from his brow with his sleeve, he looked over to Roy. "I'm sure I could do that. How old are the shingles?"

A deep smile set into Roy's face as he thought about when he and his father had built the barn back when he was just a boy. "It's been forty years now." His father had always taken a fancy to his older brother, but when his brother had gone away on a mission trip for the summer, his dad had relied on Roy for help with constructing the barn. Delighted, he'd spent the summer toiling in the heat with his dad. He helped lay the foundation, paint the barn and even helped put on the roof. Through sharing the heat of summer and sips of lemonade that his mother would bring out to them, Roy and his father grew close, and remained that way until his father's death later in life.

"Forty years is a while... my dad re-shingled his barn after twenty."

"Shingles usually last between twenty and thirty years." Roy paused to let out a short laugh. "I've been pushing it for ten. Really should have done it last summer when I first started seeing the leaks, but I hadn't the strength and was still too stubborn to accept your help around here."

"I imagine it's quite difficult to admit needing help. I don't envy growing old –no offense."

"None taken," Roy replied, glancing over his shoulder at the sound of a car coming up the driveway over the bridge. "I believe my grandchildren have arrived."

"I'll be on my way then; I don't want to keep you, and it seems to me we are done here."

"Thank you for the help today. I'll write your check, but first get the hay conveyor equipment put away. Just come inside the farmhouse when you're done."

Roy climbed down the ladder and Levi followed behind him. As Roy exited the barn doors, he could see his daughter faintly behind the reflection of the sun off the windshield of her silver Prius. Love overcame him as he made eye contact with her. His daughter was the apple of his eye, and he felt she was the only thing he had done right in all the years of his life on earth. He'd never admit it to anyone out loud, but Tiff was his favorite child. She was the first-born and held a special place in his heart. The other kids gravitated more to their mother anyway; Tiffany and he were always close.

Parking in front of the garage that matched the paint of the barn, red with white trim, His daughter Tiffany stepped out of the driver side door and smiled at him. Hurrying her steps through the gravel, she ran up to her dad and hugged him as she let out what seemed to be a sigh of relief.

Watching over her shoulder as Jess got out of the car, Roy saw her slam the door. He suspected the drive hadn't gone that well for the three of them, but did the courtesy of asking without assuming. "How was the drive?"

"You don't want to ask..." she replied, glancing back at Jess as her daughter lingered near the corner of the garage.

Roy smiled. "I have a fresh batch of lemonade inside," he said, trying to lighten the tension he could sense. Seeing Henry was still in the backseat fiddling with something, Roy went over to one of the back doors and opened the door.

"Hi Grandpa," Henry said, looking up at him.

Leaning his head into the car, Roy smiled. "I'm looking for Henry, have you seen him? Because there's no way you are, Henry! He's just a little guy." Roy used his hand to show how tall Henry *should be* and continued, "About this tall, if my memory serves me correctly."

Henry laughed. "Stop Grandpa! It's me, I'm Henry!"

"I know... I'm just playing with you, kiddo! I haven't seen you in years! You've grown like a weed! Give your ol' Grandpa a hug!" Henry dropped his tablet on the seat and climbed over a suitcase of Jess's to embrace his grandpa in a warm hug.

"Can we go fishing Grandpa? Can we go today?"

Roy laughed as he stood upright. "Maybe tomorrow. The day is going to be over soon and I'd like to visit with your mother some."

Henry dipped his chin to his chest as he sighed. "Okay." Reaching into the back trunk area of the car, Henry grabbed his backpack and then scooted off his seat and out from the car. Just then, Jess let out a screech, which directed everyone's attention over to her at the garage.

"A mouse, are you kidding me?" With a look of disgust, she stomped off around Levi's truck, and down the sidewalk that led up to the farmhouse.

"Aren't you forgetting something?" Tiffany asked, which caused Jess to stop in her tracks. She turned around and put her hand over her brow to shield the sun.

"What, mom?"

"Your suitcases... maybe?" Tiffany replied with a sharp tone.

Roy placed a hand on Tiffany's shoulder. "That's okay. Henry and I can get them."

"No. Jess needs to get them." Roy could tell that his daughter was attempting to draw a line in the sand. A line that Roy and his late wife Lucille had drawn many times with her and the kids.

"Really, Mom?" Jess asked, placing a hand on her hip. "Those suitcases are heavy; the men should carry them. Grandpa is right."

Henry tugged on his mother's shirt corner. "I think you should let this one go, Mother." He smiled and nodded to Roy. "Grandpa and I have it."

Tiffany shook her head and turned away

from Jess as she went to the back of the car. "She's so difficult, Dad. I hate it," Tiffany said, slapping the trunk. "She doesn't understand how life really works."

"Winnie," Roy replied. "Pick your battles." The nickname *Winnie* came from when she was three years old. She would wake up in the middle of the night, push a chair up to the pantry and sneak the honey back into her bedroom. On several occasions, they would awaken the next day to find her snuggling an empty bottle of honey underneath her covers.

"I know. It's just hard sometimes, because everything is a battle with her lately."

"She'll come around. You just have to give her some time to process everything."

Chapter 3 ~ Jess

Kicking her shoes off on the front patio, Jess noticed a hummingbird feeder hanging from the roof's corner. A small bird was zipping around the feeder frantically. She smiled as she thought of her friend Troy, back in Seattle. He was a boxer and often referred to himself as the hummingbird.

Entering into the farmhouse, Jess glanced around and saw that nothing had changed since she had been there five years ago. The same two beige couches with the squiggly designs on the fabric sat in the living room, one couch on each side. The same pictures of all the family hung behind the television. And even the picture of her grandmother, Lucille, which sat on the mantle above the fireplace, right between the wooden praying hands and the shelf clock. Everything was the same.

Walking up to the picture of her grandma, she looked at it longingly. *Why can't mom be like you were, Grandma?*

Hearing Henry and the rest just outside on the patio, Jess quickly made her way across the living room, through the dining room and through the door leading up the stairwell to her room she knew she'd be staying in. The wood paneling on both sides of the hallway leading upstairs made her laugh. *He has the money from Grandma's life insurance, yet he updates nothing.* It was so old and outdated, but then again, everything was in the house.

Lying down on the daybed that was pushed up against the lone window in the room, she turned on her side and peered out the window. Pushing the curtain back, she could see down the hillside and a faint view through the trees of the creek. She couldn't help but recall playing in it with Henry and all her cousins, years ago.

They would sneak pots and pans from the kitchen when grandma wasn't looking and journey down the hillside with them to the creek. They were *farming for gold* as they often referred to it. Looking back over her childhood, she couldn't help but have a longing for the simpler times. Grandma was alive, mom and dad were together and all the cousins lived in the same city. She hated being forced by her mother's hand to be at the farm this summer, but she loved the childhood memories that came with being there.

Hearing the door open at the base of the stairwell, Jess slid off the bed. She suspected her mother was going to be calling for her.

"Come down and visit with your grandpa," her mother hollered up the stairs loudly. Jess came out of the room and looked down the stairs at her mom.

"You don't have to yell..."

"Just come downstairs and visit, please." Her mother left the door open and walked away. *It was hot up here anyway.* Jess missed a step on her way down the stairs and tumbled to the bottom.

"Ooouuuchhh!" Jess said, grabbing onto the arm that she had braced herself with on the fall. Glancing up, she was greeted by laughter from a rude, but very attractive, brown-haired boy with the bluest eyes she'd ever seen.

Extending a hand to help her up, he said, "I'm sorry, but that was just too funny."

Jess pushed his hand out of her way. "I'm glad my pain can be of entertainment to you." Pushing herself up off the steps, she stood up and looked at him. "Who are you?" she asked curiously.

"I'm Levi. I live up the road and help Roy out with the farm. I know you're Roy's granddaughter, but I didn't catch your name...?"

"I'm Jess... I had no idea other people lived out here our age. How do you stand to live without cell phones and cable?"

"What's a cell phone?" Levi laughed. "I'm

only kidding. You just get used to it." Jess nodded as she proceeded past him.

Entering into the kitchen, she grabbed for a clean glass from the dish rack and poured herself a glass of ice water. Taking a drink, she looked over to the table to see Henry, her mother and grandpa all staring at her.

"What?" she asked.

"Don't be *rude* with your tone Missy," her mom said. "But are you okay? We heard you fall down the stairs."

Jess's back and arm were hurting a little from falling, but she didn't want to let her mother get the satisfaction of nurturing her. "I'm fine, Mom."

"Ok. Well, your Grandfather and Henry are going to fish over on Long Lake tomorrow morning; did you want to join them?"

Jess immediately thought of her dad. In fact, every time she heard the word *fish* since the split, she'd think of him. Even the stupid commercials on television that were just ads for fishing supply businesses triggered it. She and her father would go on fishing trips at least twice a month during the summer, and sometimes even more. Last year, they had entered a fishing competition on Lake Roosevelt and had won first place. They got a trophy and a cash prize. It put them that much closer to their dream of getting a *real* fishing boat, instead of the duct-taped-up aluminum canoe they had gotten as a hand-me-down from Roy. It barely floated.

She was already upset that she had to be at the farm all summer; she wasn't going to give her grandpa or mother the satisfaction of her going fishing with him. They knew she enjoyed fishing, and that'd be a win for their column. "No." She turned to her grandpa and narrowed her look at him. "I won't be fishing at all this summer. I'll wait for dad to get back to do my fishing." Taking another drink of her water, she finished it and slammed the cup down in her frustration, and then exited the kitchen, angered she'd been even asked to go fishing.

Jess knew her grandpa most likely had some hand in her mother's decision to walk out on her father, and it infuriated Jess. He always had a dislike for Jess's dad. Jess thought it had to do with the day when the three of them had all gone fishing together and her grandpa never got as much as a bite on his hook. Yet her dad, in all his awesomeness, reeled in three that same day.

On her way back to the stairs, she saw into the living room that her luggage had been brought in. Unfortunately, the rude boy was sitting on a couch near her luggage. *Oh great, another encounter with prince charming.* As she grabbed her bags, he lowered his newspaper and looked at her beaming with a smile.

"Why do you insist on smiling constantly?"

"I'm happy."

"I find that hard to believe. You live in the middle of nowhere and have, like, no life." Levi kept the smile on his face and brought the paper back up to read. Jess felt like she was a bit harsh with him. "I'm sorry. I didn't mean that. I'm just... really upset right now. Sorry."

"You don't even know me or my life. You're just a city brat and I'm just a country hick, so let's just keep our distance from each other."

"You think I'm a brat?"

"No, I don't think you are..."

"Good..."

"No, let me finish. I know you are a brat." He lowered his paper and glanced at her. "The way you carried on in there with your grandpa was horrible. I wouldn't be caught dead talking to anyone that way, let alone my own grandfather."

Jess shook her head with her tongue in cheek. "You know what? You're right. Let's keep our distance from each other."

Levi raised his paper back up to read, and she scowled at him. Her grandpa came into the living room and said, "Levi."

Setting his paper down, he stood up and walked into the kitchen with her grandpa. Her mom noticed the tension between them as she and Henry came in and sat on the opposite couch from Jess.

"What's that all about?"

"Nothing, Mom. Just a country boy living in a bubble."

"What happened?"

"Well... he laughed at me for falling, for starters."

Henry snickered.

"Stop that," her mom said to Henry.

"And then... he called me a brat."

Her mom couldn't help from smiling, but she covered her face in the attempts to hide it. "I'm sorry, dear... You should try to get along with him though; he's been helping your Grandpa a lot out here."

Jess sighed, shaking her head. *I should have*

just taken that offer of Tragan's. That would have made more sense than being here. "Sure, Mom," Jess replied, rolling her eyes. She and Tragan, her friend in Seattle, were going to room together after Jess had learned of the *summer at grandpa's* idea of her mom's. She figured she was eighteen and could do whatever she wanted; her mom couldn't stop her. But after looking into the cost of splitting rent on a two-bedroom apartment in Seattle, she decided against it. There was no way she would be able to finish her senior year, spend time with her friends and work all at the same time, so she elected to obey her mother. Thinking back on it now, she wondered if she had made the right choice.

Chapter 4 ~ Roy

Standing up from the kitchen table, Roy extended his hand and shook Levi's firmly. Every week, after writing him a check, they'd shake on it. There was no need for contracts or other paperwork miscellanies out in the back country. The people out there were trusted and relied on by their word and their handshake.

"Be sure to tell your father hello for me." Roy retrieved a pocket watch from his pants' pocket and placed it in Levi's hands. On the face, it had an etching of a train stopping to let people on, and the exterior was entirely made of gold. "I want you to have this. I picked it up from the flea market the other day, and when I saw it, I thought of you."

"What about it made you think of me?" Levi asked.

"Life is kinda like a train. Sometimes it stops; sometimes it goes, but along the way it's always on track going somewhere. When my train had stopped, you were there to hop on."

"I'm sorry, but that sounds quite ridiculous."

"Ridiculous or not, I want you to have it."

"I can't take this," Levi said, rubbing the

surface before trying to hand it back to Roy.

"Please take it. I'll be offended if you don't. Now, don't forget to tell your father hello for me."

"I will, sir. It's always a pleasure working with you." Heading for the side door that led out of the kitchen and into the porch, Levi turned to Roy. "You have your work cut out this summer with that girl."

Roy smiled. "I know." Patting him on the back, Roy said, "That's why I have God to help me." Levi nodded and proceeded out into the porch, shutting the door behind him.

Walking through the kitchen, Roy could hear his daughter and grandchildren conversing about him in the living room. Stopping, he leaned against the doorway and listened.

Jess laughed. "He belongs in a home. You know it, I know it... we all have known it since Grandma passed. It's just ridiculous that he's draining his retirement paying that stupid boy."

She sure doesn't like him.

"My dad isn't going to give up this farm, Jess, that's just the way it is. This farm is in his blood. Without it, who knows how long he'd hold on. Meadows down the block from our house in Seattle would be perfect for him... but I don't see it ever happening, and I don't know if I want it to, either."

Roy sighed heavily as he leaned against the door frame. *She's already looked into it?* As if the next minute aged him fifty years, Roy found himself exhausted. Going back into the kitchen, he took a seat at the table and glanced out the large kitchen windows that overlooked the front yard. He watched as Levi walked the sidewalk out to his truck.

"Grandpa?" Henry said, walking into the kitchen.

"Yes?"

"Do you miss your dad?" Henry asked, as he climbed up to a seat at the table. Reaching across the table, he snatched an apple from the bowl of fruit.

"Every day," Roy replied. Over the years it had gotten easier for Roy, not because he'd missed his fatherless, but because he'd learned to live with a hole in his life.

"I miss my dad... a lot," Taking a bite of his apple, Henry had a smile crawl on his face. "He should be back in town when we get back to Seattle though, so it's not *too* far from now."

Roy rubbed Henry's head as he ignored the

comment about Brandon entirely. "Are you ready to go fishing tomorrow?" Henry nodded as he took another bite of his apple. "How big of fish are you going to catch?"

Henry leaped up from his chair. Stretching one arm up as high as he could reach, he said, "This big!"

"Ha," Jess said, walking into the kitchen to the fridge. Opening the door to the fridge, she sighed heavily. Roy didn't keep much food that the kids would enjoy around the house; he had forgotten to fetch some for their visit. That was something that Lucille had always taken care of before the grandchildren would arrive.

"There's soda on the porch, I know how you kids don't enjoy lemonade much," Roy smiled, hoping it would be good enough.

Jess shut the fridge and opened the door leading into the porch. Leaning, she looked out and laughed. "Diet caffeine-free..."

Henry cringed as he heard his sister. "Gross, Grandpa."

"I'm sorry about that. We can get some food and stuff tomorrow. Henry and I will be sure to swing by the grocery store on the way back from fishing."

Jess was going to leave the kitchen, but stopped and looked at her grandpa. "There's really nothing to do out here."

"You could go for a walk on the hill, read, paint, and draw... Really, anything is possible out here if you put your mind to it."

"Cell phones and cable aren't possible, no matter how much you put your mind to it."

"That's true, but those things are just distractions. You have to embrace life out here without all that technology."

"Whatever," Jess said, rolling her eyes as she walked out to the porch.

"She stresses mom out," Henry said, looking intently at his grandpa. "We don't know what to do with her."

Laughing, Roy said, "Who's *we*?"

"Mom and I."

Roy furrowed his eyebrows. "You're ten years old. You don't need to worry about Jess. She's not your concern. That's your mom's territory." Henry nodded and got down from the table. Watching as Henry walked out of the kitchen, sadness overtook Roy. Henry was but a child, and he was attempting to fill a void that only a father could. Roy knew he had a long summer ahead of him, but more importantly, he knew God had a plan in the midst of the chaos and turmoil in those two children's lives.

Looking out the window at the chicken coop across the yard, Roy watched as Jess ventured over to it. It reminded him of Tiffany's fascination with the chicken coop when she was but a child. Back years ago when she was six, she'd go out every morning before breakfast and collect all the eggs. While she didn't have a fondness for the smells that resided in the chicken coop, she loved those chickens and hens dearly.

"How many hens do you have now?" Tiffany asked, coming into the kitchen and leaning her head over Roy's shoulder.

"We have twelve," Roy replied with a smile, watching Jess open the door and go in.

Tiffany took a seat at the table and Roy turned to her. "She's not as lost as you think she is, Winnie."

"You don't know how difficult it is..." Tiffany said, putting her hands to her forehead as she rested her elbows on the table. "She doesn't listen to anything I say, Dad, and she hates everyone and everything except her father and her friends."

Roy placed a hand on Tiffany's and brought

it away from her face. "She's just a teenager. You were there once."

"Nothing like this, Dad."

"I'm sure it's different, but it's still the same. Children go through phases in life and she's going through one right now. You add in the fact that--"

"I know," Tiffany interrupted.

Roy stood up from the table and kissed his daughter's forehead. "I love you, Winnie, and your children are going to be *okay*. Just trust that God is doing a work here."

Chapter 5 ~ Jess

Plugging her nose, Jess took one look around the chicken coop and almost vomited. Straw and feces littered the creaky wood-planked floors. Turning, she pushed the chicken coop door open and almost fell out trying to move quickly.

"Disgusting!" she shouted, tiptoeing out of the coop.

Looking across the yard, she could see her grandpa through the farmhouse kitchen windows. He was waving at her with a big silly grin on his face. She turned away and looked across the field just beyond the coop that held the herd of her grandfather's cattle. The field sat at the base of the hill. Glancing up the hill, she saw the big rocks sitting on top.

Jess and her cousin Reese would trek up the hill and sit on a particular rock, and look down across the vast and open valley. Years ago, their grandmother would pack them lunches and juice boxes to take on their journey up there. They never made it beyond the rocks before stopping to eat their lunches, and one of those rocks was where they would sit and eat every time they went. She and Reese stashed a lunch box with a few baseball cards, a couple of colorful rocks and one Pog slammer. Every summer they'd go and find the same rock and the lunch box. It was like finding treasure every time. *I wonder if it's still there.* She thought as she kept her eyes on the rocks.

Walking back over to the farmhouse, she went into the kitchen where her grandfather and mother were sitting.

"Can I borrow the car, Mom?"

Her mom looked at her phone's time and shook her head. "I need to get back on the road shortly. I am stopping in Spokane for a meal with an old friend."

"Cool mom, thanks again for abandoning us just like you did Dad..." and under her breath, she said, "I hate you." Jess began to leave the kitchen.

"Just a minute there, girl! That's not respectful of your mother. If you could be a bit nicer you might be able to take my work truck," Roy said.

Jess stopped, frozen in her tracks. It was a pivotal moment for her. She had to decide whether or not to accept the offer from her grandpa. On one hand, she knew that she *needed* a vehicle if she was going anywhere this summer, and that meant using her grandpa's truck. On the other hand, she didn't want to give him the satisfaction of helping her. She didn't want him thinking that his involvement in her mom and dad's split was okay or justified. She was torn.

"Really?" Jess asked. She couldn't come up with anything else to spit out.

"Yep."

"Ok..." Jess said, walking back into the kitchen. She decided to take the generous offer, but she wasn't going to be happy about it. Her eyes searched the counters for a set of keys. "Where are the keys?"

"How about an apology? To your mother?" Roy asked.

Jess's jaw clenched and she could feel her blood begin to boil as she tried to keep herself from screaming. Turning slowly to her mother, she smiled forcefully. "I'm sorry, Mother."

"And what about *me* being kind enough to use the truck?"

Jess's teeth ground a bit while she tried to keep the smile. Without opening her mouth, and through her teeth, she said, "Thank you... Where are the keys?"

"Right there," Roy said, pointing to the counter. There was a stack of mail, a screw driver and some magazines.

"I'm not seeing them."

"The screwdriver," Roy said with a laugh.

"Ohhh...." Jess forced another smile. "I see."

"You don't have to drive it if you don't want to. I'm just offering it. It ain't a beauty by no means."

"No, I understand... I want to drive it." Jess grabbed the screwdriver and darted out of the kitchen. Leaving the farmhouse, she walked quickly along the path out towards the garage when her grandpa opened the window from the kitchen.

"The truck is along side of the barn," Roy hollered.

"Thanks!" Jess shouted over her shoulder. *Ugh... I didn't have to thank him again.*

Coming to the barn, Jess found that the barn doors were opened and she ventured in for a moment. Looking up at the rafters, she was filled with a familiar feeling that had been lost in her childhood. Back then she had such little care for life and the problems of the real world, like high school. Glancing over to the upper loft of the barn, she saw hay bales and recalled building forts with her cousins. They'd stack bales that reached almost to the ceiling of the barn.

Snapping herself out of the memories, she

turned and left the barn, headed for the truck that was parked along the side. When she got to the truck's door, she couldn't get the door open. Kicking it, she began to scream in her frustration. It was so hot outside she could barely hold onto the handle to open the truck for more than a moment. "Come on!"

"Calm down," Henry said coming around the corner of the barn. "You sound like you are being killed, Jess."

"Shut it, twerp."

"Let me help." Henry came up beside Jess.

"Ha. I'd like to see you try," she replied, stepping out of the way of Henry.

Henry gave each of his hands a spit and rubbed them together. *Gross.* She watched as her brother used all his force in the attempts to dislodge the truck door's handle. It was useless. He stopped and began to look around, spotting a wooden rake stuck in the ground as if it had been there for a very long time.

"You are going to rake the truck?" Jess asked jokingly.

Henry remained silent as he dislodged the rake from the ground. It appeared to have sunk partially into the grass and dirt in the field. Brushing off the dirt, Henry came back to the truck and used the butt of the rake to jam it up into the door handle.

"Good try, but I don't—" Suddenly the door popped open. Henry stood proudly with his chest puffed out. "Thanks," Jess said.

"Pleasure helping you, madam."

"Trying to talk like a cowboy," Jess said with a laugh. "Even Grandpa doesn't talk like that."

Henry beamed. "It's fun to pretend."

"I'm sure it is; I use to do the same thing when I was younger. Thanks bro." Pretending and dolls use to be a huge part of Jess's life. All the way up until she hit ninth grade and Suzie Donaldson came over to visit after school one day. Jess could recall it like it had just happened. When Suzie came over, she had laughed at Jess's doll collection. That marked the turning point for Jess. She wasn't going to be a little kid who played with dolls anymore; she was going to be a *cool kid* like Suzie, and leave the dolls behind.

Jess climbed into the truck and shoved the screwdriver into the ignition. After turning the screwdriver over, the truck fired up loudly and she pumped the gas to get it going. "Yay..." she said sarcastically as she began pulling forward around the front of the barn.

"I wanna go, I wanna go!" Henry shouted as he ran alongside the truck.

"I'd love to let you... but I can't." Jess drove off, leaving Henry in the rearview mirror as she went down the driveway, over the bridge, and out onto Elk Chattaroy Road.

Did you enjoy this preview?
*Pick up a copy of **The Perfect Cast** today!*

OTHER BOOKS

Embers & Ashes Series

Amongst the Flames (Book 1)

Out of the Ashes (Book 2)

Up in Smoke (Book 3)

After the Fire (Book 4)

Love's Enduring Promise Series

The Perfect Cast (Book 1)

Finding Love (Book 2)

Claire's Hope (Book 3)

Dylan's Faith (Book 4)

Stand Alones

Love Again (Re-released 12/3/2015)

Love Interrupted

A Chance at Love (Coming Early 2016)

The Lost Truth (Coming 2016)

Visit www.tkchapin.com for all the latest releases

Subscribe to the Newsletter for special

Prices, free gifts and more!

www.tkchapin.com

AUTHOR'S NOTE

When you leave a review on a book you read, you're helping the author keep the lights on. Our books don't sell themselves, it's word of mouth and comments others have made. Simply visit Amazon and/or Goodreads and let others know how the book was for you. It'd help me greatly. Thank you!

ABOUT THE AUTHOR

T.K. CHAPIN writes Christian Romance books designed to inspire and tug on your heart strings. He believes that telling stories of faith, love and family help build the faith of Christians and help non-believers see how God can work in the life of believers. He gives all credit for his writing and storytelling ability to God. The majority of the novels take place in and around Spokane Washington, his hometown. Chapin makes his home in the Pacific Northwest and has the pleasure of raising his daughter with his beautiful wife Crystal. To find out more about T.K. Chapin or his books, visit his website at www.tkchapin.com.

Made in the
USA
Columbia, SC